How Ali Ferguson
Saved Houdini

Also by Elen Caldecott

How Kirsty Jenkins Stole the Elephant

HOW Ali FERGUSON SAVED HOUDINI

ELEN CALDECOTT

BLOOMSBURY

LONDON BERLIN NEW YORK

First published in Great Britain in July 2010 by Bloomsbury Publishing Plc
36 Soho Square, London, W1D 3QY

A CIP catalogue record of this book is available from the British Library

ISBN 978 1 4088 0574 9

FSC
Mixed Sources
Product group from well-managed
forests and other controlled sources
Cert no. SGS - COC - 2061
www.fsc.org
© 1996 Forest Stewardship Council

Typeset by Dorchester Typesetting Group Ltd
Printed in Great Britain by Clays Ltd, St Ives Plc, Bungay, Suffolk

1 3 5 7 9 10 8 6 4 2

www.bloomsbury.com/elencaldecott

For all my different parents,
especially Mum

CHAPTER 1

'Cool!' Ali looked up at the skyscraper that was his new home.

'Ali,' Mum said, smiling, 'it's just a tower block, not the Empire State Building.'

'Yes, but it's *our* tower block!' Ali said. 'Do you think it has a lift?'

'Go and find out. We're number 22.' Mum threw him the keys.

Ali caught them with one hand and ran up the steps. A man stepped out of the main door before Ali had a chance to unlock it. Ali nearly ran full tilt into his chest. He was a tall man, with a shaved head and a tattoo of a bluebird flying up his neck. One of the new neighbours. Scary-looking.

'All right, sonny. Where's the fire?' the man said with a laugh that showed a gold tooth.

'Sorry,' Ali said, then lowered his head and ran into the foyer.

Inside, a tiled floor, summer-sky blue, stretched out as far as the lift. On one wall was a noticeboard where colourful posters fluttered like prayer flags.

Lever Tower. His new home. There was just something about the air that made Ali's heart beat faster. This was a new adventure.

For two years, since Dad left, he'd been living with Mum in Nan and Grandpa's house. But now, they had their own place. In a skyscraper! With the river and the sea just behind it! This was going to be brilliant!

Behind Ali, the neighbour held the main door open while the others came inside. Grandpa carried a suitcase in each hand. He was muttering to himself.

Ali grinned and took one of the cases. 'Isn't it great, Grandpa?'

Grandpa scowled.

Mum and Nan both carried huge boxes. 'Did you find it yet?' Mum asked.

'No. Give me a chance!' Ali laughed as he pressed the lift call button.

The lift whirred into life.

'At least it doesn't smell,' Mum said to Grandpa. Grandpa didn't reply.

They went up to the fourth floor. Number 22 was

the third door on the left. Ali unlocked it and stepped inside.

The hallway was narrow. Bright winter sunlight spilled into it from the living room beyond. Ali pushed open all the doors as he went: bathroom; kitchen; big bedroom; little bedroom and then the living room. 'You can have the big room, Mum!' he shouted.

'Very kind of you, thanks,' Mum said.

Grandpa came in slowly, looking at everything. He spoke in Gujarati to Mum. She could understand, but didn't really speak it. Ali could hardly understand any. But he guessed that, most likely, Grandpa was complaining about the poor craftsmanship of the door, or the wonkiness of the windows, or how the whole thing was bound to collapse any second. He and Nan hadn't wanted Ali and Mum to move here. There were rumours about gangs and criminals and all sorts of trouble. One local girl had even stolen from the museum last year!

Ali thought that was pretty cool, but he hadn't said so to Grandpa.

'Don't worry, Dad. We're going to be fine here.' Mum gave Grandpa a quick hug. 'It was high time we stopped getting under your feet. I think we all need a cup of tea.'

'No problem,' Nan shouted from the kitchen.

'There was no way I'd put the kettle in storage. I've got it right here. Tea's on its way.'

Tea? Ali shook his head. He and Mum were at the start of a brand new adventure together and she wanted a cup of tea? Unbelievable.

Mum caught his eye and grinned. 'Why don't you go and explore a bit, love? Have a look at your room. The furniture won't be here until later. You can decide where it's going to go.'

Ali didn't need a second invitation.

His new room was smallish, but there would be enough space for his bed, a wardrobe and desk. And a shelf for his books. He moved over to the window. The trees waved their bare branches just below him. Ali was actually looking down on them – down on to the tops of the trees! It was like rising up in a hot air balloon, floating over the town. Way below he could see the yard where Grandpa had parked and the racks where his bike could go later. There was hardly anyone about down there, but one person caught Ali's eye, a girl being dragged along by a huge dog. She held the lead with both hands and leaned backwards, as though she was water-skiing. The dog was an Alsatian. It leapt forwards, pulling on the lead. Ali could see the girl's mouth move as she yelled at the dog, but he was too high up to hear her. He grinned. He was pretty sure that whatever she was saying, it was rude.

He suddenly wanted to be outside with them too, in the crisp air, with the frozen grass crunching under his feet.

'Mum?' he yelled.

'Yes?' Her voice came from the kitchen next door.

'Can I explore outside?'

'Yes. But don't go too far, OK? And don't be too long – we've got some serious unpacking to do.'

'Thanks!'

He grabbed the keys from the top of the hall storage heater and then he ran out the front door.

He ignored the lift and found the stairs. He took them three at a time, his feet launching high off the concrete. At the end of each flight he used the banister as a pivot, swinging round to leap down the next set. In no time at all, he was at the bottom. A little out of breath, warmer, and ready to see this new world. He pushed open the main door.

The girl was gone. The yard was empty. The dog must have been pulling her at fifty miles an hour! Ali looked around. Grass grew on either side of the yard. He could see fresh tracks where feet had squashed the blades. One small set and then another set of massive paws. A trail to follow.

Immediately, Ali was a tracker following his quarry.

He raised his hand to halt the expedition party behind him. He heard the clang of billy-cans clattering and silently cursed the clumsy lumps behind him. He crouched to examine the paw prints. They were clear and distinct in the grass. Leading off into the unknown. 'Follow me,' he whispered to the team behind him. 'Stay downwind. Don't let the pack pick up your scent.'

He led his team away from the main door, around the side of Lever Tower. Always he kept his head down, eyes following the tracks, searching out the path the animal took. Sometimes the path was clear – deep furrows in the ground where the beast must have pulled the girl right over. Sometimes the trail was nothing more than an icy blade of grass bent out of shape.

He heard whispers from his team. They could see nothing at all. They admired his skill. He hushed them with a wave of his hand.

He followed the trail left, then left, then left again.

He was back outside the main entrance to the tower block.

And there were fresh sets of prints on the tarmac leading up to the front door.

The girl had just walked around the outside of Lever Tower and then gone right back inside again! Well, he thought, if he were walking a dog the size of a bear, he'd only take it for a short walk too.

He raced up the path and through the door. He stopped in the foyer.

He had the trail – he knew he could find them easily – but was that really such a good idea? He couldn't follow a total stranger to her flat! Stalking people was no way to make friends. He would see the girl and her massive dog again, he was sure.

He'd have to explore something else instead.

He'd been all around the tower. Now it was time to explore *up* the tower. Scaling unknown heights. Like Tenzing Norgay – one of Grandpa's all-time heroes – climbing Everest!

Ali checked his supplies – rope, thermal clothing, mountain rations. Well, a bit of string in his pockets, one glove and a mint humbug. It was good enough. He set off from base camp and began his ascent, counting the steps as he went.

'One, two, three, four . . .'

'. . . Twenty-six, twenty-seven . . .'

'. . . Ninety-three . . . ninety-four . . . ninety-five.'

At a snowy ledge on step one hundred and twenty-eight, Ali sat down to rest, muttering 'hundred and twenty-eight, hundred and twenty-eight,' over and over, so that he wouldn't lose count. As soon as he had got used to the thin air, he broke camp and battled on.

'Hundred and eighty-seven, hundred and eighty-eight . . .'

'. . . Two hundred and eleven, two hundred and twelve.'

He was panting now, clinging to every handhold to help him climb.

'. . . Two hundred and fifty, two hundred and fifty-one, two hundred and fifty-two!' He was finally at the summit. He rested his hands on his knees, gasping for breath. He had made it – Tenzing Norgay on top of the world!

Then he realised he was not quite at the top. Further on, set away from the main staircase, were five steps, leading upwards to a doorway. The door had a big red sign on it: 'Authorised Personnel Only'. But the door was ajar.

CHAPTER 2

Ali pushed the door open. The wind hit him first. A roaring wind that whipped his hood back and stole his breath away. This was the true summit of the mountain. He stepped out. Icy gusts swirled around him, straight from the snowcapped peaks of the Himalayas.

He raised his head, fighting the elements, tears swimming in his eyes.

He was standing right in the middle of the roof! Right on the very top of Lever Tower.

If only Dad could see this.

The thought came suddenly, from nowhere.

The pain was sharper and colder than the wind. Three postcards ago, Dad had been planning a trip to the Himalayas. Ali didn't know if he'd ever got there. He hadn't said in the next two cards.

Ali rubbed his eyes fiercely. Today was the start of

something new. He could imagine he was on Everest if he wanted, and it had *nothing to do with Dad*.

He ran towards the edge of the tower, leaned against the barrier and looked out at the kingdom below. The homes of the mountain villagers were like toy houses; the few people he could make out were like bugs – no, even smaller, like fleas. He could see the fields where they grew their crops, the park and the great city beyond. Well, the allotments and the town, anyway.

Cutting through it all was the river, shining and winking in the low sunlight as it moved past the warehouses towards the sea. The sea! He should be able to see it from the other side of the tower!

He raced around the concrete block that housed the doorway and the lift machinery, right to the opposite side of the roof. Below, the river flowed into the sea, about a mile away. He could see the docks huddled along the coast, and the water, hanging below the sky in a dark grey strip. A red cargo ship travelled along the horizon. The wind was at his back now, as though it could lift him off and blow him, like a seagull, over the waves.

'Hey!'

The voice came from behind him. He turned slowly. There, sheltering out of the wind in the shadow of the concrete block, was the girl he had seen earlier. And her huge dog. He had found them after all! Ali grinned. Up close, he could see that the girl must be about the same age as him. She had straggly blonde hair pulled back off her face. She was frowning. The dog stood up.

'Hello,' he said. 'Nice dog.'

The girl didn't answer.

'What's his name?' Ali asked.

'She's not a *him*. She's a *her*.'

'Oh.' So the natives were not friendly. Ali smiled at the girl. 'Is she yours?' he asked. He stepped closer, holding his hands out so that the dog could smell him if she wanted to.

Ali didn't think the girl was going to speak. Then she sighed dramatically. 'A bit yes and a bit no.'

'What do you mean?'

'We're looking after her. Me and Dad. While her real owner is away.'

Ali edged closer. The dog sniffed the air, then wagged her tail. Ali laid his hand gently on her back and started stroking. Her fur was soft and warm. 'What's her name?' he asked.

'Falcon.'

'That's a cool name for a mountain dog,' Ali said.

'What?'

'Oh. Nothing. I was just pretending that I was

climbing a mountain. Like Tenzing Norgay.'

'Who?'

Ali shrugged. 'I was just playing. What's your name?'

The girl sniffed. 'Caitlin. Caitlin Mary O'Connor.'

'I'm Ali. Ali Desai Ferguson. I've just moved here with my mum.'

'Desai?' Caitlin struggled to pronounce it. 'And I thought Tenz-whatever-it-was was a daft name. Where are you from? Pakistan?'

'No. My mum was born in Blackpool. I've never even been on holiday abroad.'

'Oh.' Caitlin paused. 'I went to France once. It was brilliant.'

Ali grinned. 'But my grandpa is Indian. Came here ages ago and met Nan.'

'And then you were born and moved here. Lucky us.'

Ali smiled. 'I like it here. I think it's exciting. Don't you?'

The girl shrugged. 'Sometimes. Just now, it's . . . odd. What floor do you live on?'

'The fourth. Flat 22. What do you mean, "odd"?' Ali asked.

She ignored his question. 'Well, I live on the *fourteenth*. It's much better than the fourth. Everyone knows that.'

Ali laughed and, amazingly, Caitlin laughed too.

'How can you look after a dog on the fourteenth floor?' Ali asked.

Caitlin's smile vanished, and her scowl was back more deeply than before. 'None of your business. In fact, I don't even know why I'm talking to you. We never talk to people, do we, Falcon?' She turned away, tugging at the lead. With Falcon following behind this time, Caitlin marched around the concrete building towards the door. The wind whipped her hair into angry tails around her head. She was out of sight. Ali heard the door slam.

Ali walked back slowly. Had he made a new friend, or a new enemy?

CHAPTER 3

Ali had his answer later that evening.

The removal men had been and delivered all the stuff that had been stored in Nan's loft for two years. The flat looked like a cardboard-box showroom. Now Ali and Mum were *trying* to get ready for their first night in their brand new home. His bed was in the right place, but Mum couldn't find sheets. She was opening boxes and cases, searching for something he could sleep under.

'Oh, Ali, look at this!' She held up a red minidress. 'I'd forgotten I even owned this. I actually used to go outdoors in this, *in public*.' She laughed. 'I wonder if I could still get into it?'

Ali grinned. He'd found some pyjamas and his toothbrush. But no sheets. There was a big beach towel on top of one of the boxes. That would do for one night. He laid it on his mattress and threw his duvet on top. He put his favourite book – his *Giant Atlas of World Animals* – on top of that. Ali lay down and let the book fall open wherever it wanted; Chapter 4: Australia. He could still hear Mum exclaiming over forgotten ornaments and pictures as she carried on unpacking in the living room. Ali read the caption under the photo of a tiger snake: 'It strikes with unerring accuracy.'

The doorbell rang.

Ali was nearest. He got up and padded barefoot to the front door. A cold draught blew from beneath it on to his toes. The peephole was too high for him to see through.

'Who's there?' he yelled.

'Ali? It's me, Caitlin.'

Ali opened the door a crack and peered out. Caitlin stood in the corridor. She was wrapped up in her thick black coat, but Ali could see the pink hem of her nightie hanging down below it. 'Hello,' he said uncertainly.

'It's Dad. He took Falcon for a walk. He does that last thing. But he hasn't come back. And that was an hour ago.'

'Oh . . . You'd best come in.'

'Will you help me look?' she asked. 'You seemed nice before. Will you help?'

'Er . . . Of course.' Ali thought Caitlin looked cross, but she sounded worried. He had to help. 'Come in. I'll have to ask my mum.'

Caitlin stepped into the hallway and Ali closed the door behind her.

'Who is it?' Mum shouted from the living room.

Ali walked ahead of Caitlin. 'Mum, this is Caitlin. She lives upstairs. Her dad went out with the dog, but he hasn't come back. Can me and Caitlin go and look for him?'

'Absolutely not!' Mum said.

Ali got ready to argue.

Then Mum grinned. 'But *me* and you and Caitlin can. Go and put something warm on. I'll grab my scarf and boots.' Mum stood up and moved towards her bedroom. As she passed Caitlin, she stopped and put a hand on her shoulder. 'Don't worry, sweetheart. We'll find him. I'm sure he just ran into a friend and lost track of time,' she said.

Caitlin nodded slowly, then gave a weak smile. 'Thanks,' she whispered.

Mum dropped a quick kiss on the top of Caitlin's head, then went into her room.

'Does your dad often stay out late?' Ali asked.

Caitlin shook her head. 'No, but like I said, odd things keep happening.'

Mum was back quickly. Ali pulled on his own coat and led the way to the lift.

Outside felt different to the way it did in the daytime. It was still and quiet, as though the cold evening mist held secrets. The street lights cast orange islands on the ground. Between the islands was the shadowy night. Parked cars were hulking shapes, and the bushes crouched in darkness. There was nobody else about. Ali zipped up his coat right to the top. 'Which way would your dad go?' he asked.

'Usually he goes round the block, as far as the foot-path to the river. There's a scrubby bit of woods there that the dogs like. Then he comes back.' Caitlin sounded much stronger now that they were actually doing something.

'Right,' Mum said. 'Let's go. Keep together, OK?'

She set off with long strides. Ali and Caitlin marched beside her. The only sounds were their own footsteps on the concrete and once, somewhere in the distance, the squeal of a van speeding away.

'Keep an eye out for any likely-looking pubs,' Mum said.

Then, out of the darkness, there came a sudden sound. Claws striking the ground. Running fast. Racing through the mist. One of the shadows, come alive and coming towards them. Ali looked left and right, trying desperately to see what it was.

'Falcon!' Caitlin dropped down on one knee as the huge dog bounded into her arms. Ali laughed nervously. The shadow was only Falcon!

Caitlin spoke urgently. 'Falcon, where's Dad? Do you know?'

'Is she like a police dog?' Ali asked.

'No, she's as thick as mince. But she *must* know where Dad is. Fetch, Falcon. Fetch! Find Dad!'

Falcon sat. Her huge mouth lolled open as she panted.

'Falcon!' Caitlin said impatiently.

'Well, she'll never be Lassie,' Mum said. 'It looks like we're on our own. But at least we know we're going the right way. We found Falcon; we'll find your dad.'

They carried on walking. The road narrowed as it got closer to the river. It was hardly more than a lane now. Ali saw a wooden sign marked 'Public Footpath' pointing in the direction they were walking. He realised that soon the lane would shrink down to a path. A dark, damp path, with trees looming in on either side. He shivered.

And then, in the shadows, he saw something.

'What's that?' He pointed towards the shape on the ground. Something large, something still.

'Dad!' Caitlin ran forward. Mum and Ali chased

after her. Caitlin dropped down next to the man.

Ali recognised him. His head was shaved and the dark smear of his tattoo spread up his neck. He was the man who'd held the door open that morning. The one who'd called Ali 'sonny'. His eyes were closed and a bruise had swollen up on his left cheek.

'Dad? Dad, can you hear me?'

His eyelids flickered weakly. He groaned.

'Dad? Are you hurt?'

'My head,' he moaned. He tried to lift his arm, but it seemed too heavy. It fell back to his side and his eyes closed tight again.

Mum eased Caitlin aside, gently. 'Let me look, love. What's his name?'

'David. Dave,' Caitlin said.

'Dave? Dave, if you can hear me, then open your eyes. Don't try to speak.'

Dave's eyes opened slowly.

'Don't worry. It's all going to be all right. We'll get you to a doctor. Do you think you can move?'

Dave reached up again. This time his hand made it to his head. He grabbed Mum's shoulder with his other hand and pulled himself up. Mum helped him to sit.

'What happened, Dad? Did you bang your head? Did you fall over?'

'Nothing,' he whispered. 'Nothing happened.'

19

'Dad! Something must have happened!'

'Caitlin, please! Help me get home.' Dave struggled to stand, leaning heavily on Mum and Caitlin as he did.

'You need to go to hospital, get checked out,' Mum said.

'No. I need to get home to bed. Least said, soonest mended, OK?'

'But . . .' Mum didn't sound sure. Ali could see the line between her eyebrows that meant she was unhappy. He felt unhappy too. Surely Dave needed to see a doctor?

Caitlin nudged him in the ribs. 'Help me get Dad home,' she said.

'Quickly,' Dave whispered.

Mum nodded reluctantly. Then, together, they held Dave up as he took step after painful step back to his flat.

CHAPTER 4

Ali got up early the next day. The previous night felt a bit like a dream. Being out in the misty night; finding Dave; half carrying him back to Caitlin's flat. And then, instead of sending Ali straight to bed, Mum had wrapped him up in a duvet on the couch while she made hot chocolate for them both. They drank the chocolate and talked about whether they should have called an ambulance after all. It had taken ages before they were able to go to sleep. Nothing this interesting had ever happened at Nan and Grandpa's.

Once Ali was dressed, he left a quick note for Mum. With a piece of buttered toast in one hand and his keys in the other, he left the flat and took the lift up to the fourteenth floor. He tapped lightly on Caitlin's door.

'Oh, it's you,' Caitlin said when she answered his knock. She flattened down her hair, then scowled.

Ali took one last bite of his toast, just leaving a little 'L' of crust. Falcon padded quietly to the door, wagging her tail. 'Hey!' Ali said. 'She's being friendly. I think she likes me.'

'I told you, she's thick.'

'Can I feed her the crust?'

Caitlin shrugged.

'Sit!' Ali said, holding out the toast.

Falcon looked at him, her head cocked on one side. Then, with a little shuffle of her back legs, she sat.

'No way!' Caitlin said. 'She's never done that before. She really must like you.'

Ali held out the crust and patted the top of Falcon's head as she took it. 'How's your dad?'

'Asleep. Come in if you want.'

Caitlin led the way into the living room. It was the same shape as Ali's, but with more furniture, beanbags and cushions on the floor filling the space. Two terriers lay curled up on a pile of old newspapers, one resting its chin on a headline about a local crime lord.

'How many dogs have you got?' Ali asked. Falcon – and now two more – all in one flat seemed like three too many.

'None,' Caitlin replied.

'Ha ha, very funny.'

'No, really. None. None of them belong to us. I told

you yesterday – Dad just looks after them when people are away, on holiday and stuff. We're cheaper than kennels. And more fun too. Those two are Laurel and Hardy. Their owner's coming back today.'

'So where's Falcon's owner?'

'Miss Osborne? She's always on holiday. She's got tonnes of money. She goes around in bright orange tops and zebra prints, stuff like that. She's a bit weird.' Caitlin shrugged. 'We look after Falcon loads.'

Ali smiled. How amazing was that, to go on holiday all the time? Perhaps Miss Osborne wasn't just travelling, perhaps she was making discoveries. Perhaps she was, right now, this minute, discovering new species in the rainforest or tracking rare creatures across the plains.

'She's in Spain just now,' Caitlin said, cutting through his daydream.

Oh, Spain, Ali thought. It was hardly the Amazon. Still, perhaps she was saving endangered lizards, or something.

'Why are you here, anyway?' Caitlin frowned.

Ali shook his head. He had never met anyone as rude as Caitlin before. After all, she had come round to their flat, practically in the middle of the night, and asked for their help and then, in the morning, it was as though they were strangers again! 'I just came to see how your dad was, that's all. Did he say what happened?'

Caitlin bit her lower lip. 'No, he wouldn't tell me. He just kept saying that he was OK.'

'What do you think happened? Did he get sick and faint, or . . . or something?'

'No. He's never sick. And he'd tell me if he was. I think someone hurt him. On purpose.'

'No! Really?' Ali sat down on a beanbag, the beans sliding around beneath him. 'Why? Does your dad have enemies?'

'No!' Caitlin said frowning. 'Well, no, not really. Some people gossip. But it's not true what they say. I think it's because of the way he looks.'

'What do you mean?'

Caitlin looked at him as though he was daft. 'I mean that people are thick. Just because Dad's got tattoos and muscles, they all think he must be dodgy.'

Ali thought about the way Dave looked, the tattoo, the gold tooth – he *did* look dodgy. 'But wouldn't he tell you if that's what happened? Why would he keep it secret?'

Caitlin shrugged. 'Well, he likes to think he's a hard man too. He isn't – he's sweet and kind. He's a fluffy bunny really. But he thinks he has a reputation to keep up. It scares people off. I've told him he'll never get a girlfriend if he keeps shutting people out, but he doesn't listen to me.'

Ali did his best to follow what Caitlin was saying. 'So he doesn't want you to know that someone beat him up? Because of his reputation?'

Caitlin nodded. 'I think so.'

'Is he a gangster?' Ali asked warily.

'No! I've told you! Everyone thinks he is. But they're just prejudiced. You must know what people are like. You look different too. Foreign.'

'I'm not foreign,' Ali said, bristling. 'I said. My grandpa came from India years and years and years ago. Mum was born here, and my dad comes from Glasgow. I haven't got an accent! I speak just like you! I am not foreign!'

'OK.' Caitlin grinned. 'Don't get your sari in a twist.'

Ali laughed. He couldn't help it. Caitlin was rude and prickly and difficult. But for some reason he liked her. She was funny.

'Who do you think did it?' Ali asked.

'What?'

'Hurt your dad.'

'I don't know,' she said.

'We should find out,' Ali said. He felt excited. This was a proper mystery. Day two at the flat looked as though it was going to be just as good as day one!

'How are we going to do that if Dad won't tell us?'

'We'll investigate. Come on!'

Caitlin reached for a lead. 'OK. We could go and look at where it happened. Falcon needs a walk anyway.'

At the sound of her name Falcon thumped her tail on the ground.

'Cool,' Ali said. 'Can I hold the lead?'

Outside, the mist of the night before had vanished. Now the sky was a crisp blue and the air tasted fresh. Ali let Falcon walk wherever she wanted to go. She kept her nose down, following some trail of her own.

'Look,' Ali said after a few minutes of being pulled behind the dog. 'She wants to go towards the river. She wants to investigate too.'

'She doesn't need to investigate. She was there, remember? She knows what happened. She just can't tell us, that's all,' Caitlin said.

'If only she could talk.'

'That would be weird.'

'Yes, OK, I suppose it would. We'll just have to find the clues ourselves then,' Ali said excitedly. 'We'll be like the Famous Five!'

'Yes. Except there's only two of us.'

'Well, there was only four of them. But they counted the dog too, I think. So, with Falcon, there's three of us. The Famous Three!'

They had reached the lane where they had found Dave. Ali gave a short tug on the lead and Falcon stopped pulling. It looked different in the daylight. On one side of the lane there was a narrow strip of birch trees. On the other side, the back gardens of a row of terraces. None of it looked anywhere near as spooky as it had been last night. Ali felt a bit disappointed.

'So,' he said, 'the bad guys either came from the houses or from the footpath. We can't go snooping round people's yards. We should check out the footpath for clues!'

'What kind of clues?' Caitlin asked.

'I don't know. But I bet we recognise them when we see them. Come on.'

Falcon trotted by his side as he ran to the footpath. Ali kept his eyes down on the ground, looking for anything that could lead them to the robbers, or gangsters, or . . . or . . . or *pirates* that had hurt Dave last night.

Suddenly, there was a rustling noise in the bush behind him. A boy hurled himself out of the undergrowth. Ali just had time to notice red hair and a blue tracksuit before he fell backwards into the mud with the boy's knee in his stomach.

'Gez! Get off him!' Caitlin yelled. Falcon barked, then cowered behind Caitlin.

'Smashdown!' the boy yelled in a fake American accent.

'Gez!'

The boy grinned down at Ali. He had dark green eyes like a cat's. Ali tried to breathe, but the boy's weight pinned his chest. He wriggled angrily, upsetting the boy's balance. With a quick twist Ali managed to slip his arm under the boy's leg, then he heaved upwards. The boy tottered for a minute, then crashed down on his side. Ali was up on his feet in an instant. 'Smashdown yourself!' he said.

'Gez, you're an idiot,' Caitlin said.

Gez got up off the ground, wiping a big muddy smear down the leg of his tracksuit. 'You're only saying that so he won't guess you've got a crush on me.'

'No,' Caitlin said firmly, 'I said it because you *are* an idiot.'

Gez grinned again. He reminded Ali of a rubber ball – no matter how you squished it, it just popped right back out again. 'You're new,' Gez said.

Ali nodded. He picked up Falcon's lead.

Gez looked at Caitlin. 'You're supposed to introduce us,' he said.

Caitlin rolled her eyes. 'Well, I thought you already

did that when you threw yourselves at each other. Gez, this is Ali. Ali, this is Gez. He's in my class at school. Worse luck.'

Gez ignored her. 'You didn't see me, did you? You didn't know I was watching?' He sounded eager.

'No,' Ali agreed, a bit grudgingly. 'We didn't see you.'

'We'd have run a mile if we had!' Caitlin said.

'Aw, Caitlin, don't be like that. I haven't seen you all holidays,' Gez said, grinning.

Caitlin scowled. 'Half-term only started two days ago.'

'I know. But it feels like ages. What are you two up to? Can I play?' Gez asked.

'No,' Caitlin said. 'Leave us alone, or Falcon will eat you. She's a demon dog. She eats boys for breakfast. Especially ginger ones. They taste like marmalade.'

Gez laughed. 'No, she isn't. That dog is a scaredy-cat. She's frightened of her own shadow. I've seen it!'

'No, you haven't!' Caitlin said indignantly.

'I have too! Last night.'

Ali looked across at Caitlin and gripped Falcon's lead tighter. Gez had seen something last night! They had found a witness. Well, really the witness had found them. But it amounted to the same thing. 'Where did you see Falcon last night? Was it here?'

'Shh!' Gez held a finger up to his lips. 'Not here. Not out in the open. Come on, follow me. I'll tell you everything I know.'

Gez stepped off the path, into the bushes. Ali followed, leading Falcon behind him. Caitlin came last. Ali could hear her complaining quietly about the mud on her trainers.

The bushes were a thick tangle on either side, but a narrow passage had been forced through. Gez led the way, crouched low and stepping carefully so that he hardly made a sound. Then the branches seemed to lift a little. There was a small clearing surrounded by brambles and dark, wet leaves. The clearing was just big enough for two plastic crates and a log. Gez sat down on one of the plastic crates and stretched out. 'Welcome to my office. Take a seat.' He waved towards the log. Caitlin rolled her eyes, then sat on the crate. Ali took the log. Falcon sat on the wet ground and managed to look expectant.

'So you saw Falcon last night? Was she with Dave?' Ali asked.

Gez nodded gravely.

'Well, tell us then!' Caitlin said.

'OK, OK, keep your hair on. I'll tell you.' Gez leaned in closer and began to whisper. 'It was about ten thirty. I was in my room. My mum thought I was asleep, but I wasn't. I was looking out of the window.'

'Why?' asked Ali.

'Because no one goes to bed at half ten unless they're a baby.'

That's not true, Ali thought. He would have been in bed himself if it hadn't been for Caitlin knocking on the door. 'I meant why were you looking out the window?'

Gez looked a bit embarrassed. 'Well, you see, I've been hearing this owl some nights. It hoots down by the river. You know, "Tu-whit, tu-whoo". I've never seen it, but I was looking out for it. It would be cool to see an owl, wouldn't it?'

Ali nodded. 'You know, it isn't one bird making that noise; it's two. The female bird says, "Tu-whit-tu," and then the male bird answers, "Whoo."'

'Really?' Gez was impressed. 'Do you know about birds and animals then? I used to see foxes here sometimes. Urban ones. But I haven't seen them in ages. I hope they're OK. Do foxes migrate, do you think?'

'Boys! Gez! Get to the point,' Caitlin said.

'Oh, sorry. So, I was at my window. I had the light off in the room so that I could see out better. Then I saw a man and a dog, walking down the road. That dog.' Gez pointed at Falcon, who thumped her tail on the ground.

'That was my dad. What happened next?' Caitlin leaned forward, balanced right on the edge of the crate.

'Then I saw someone else moving on the river path. I hadn't seen him at first because he'd been standing still. He was carrying something, but I couldn't see what it was. Then a van with its lights off reversed down the road. Your dad was between the van and the man on the path. They started talking. I couldn't hear what they were saying, but it made them angry. The man put down his box. He stepped right up to your dad, jabbing his finger at him. Then he punched your dad, right on the side of his head.'

Caitlin gasped.

'Your dad dropped like a stone.' Gez dropped a fist into his open palm to demonstrate. 'And that dog –' he jabbed his fingers towards Falcon – 'that dog ran away with her tail between her legs.'

Falcon whined gently.

'Then what happened?' Ali asked.

'The man who hit your dad ran up to the van. He put the box he was carrying in the back and the van drove off. Way too fast – they squealed away up the road.'

'Hey! We heard that! Do you remember?' Ali asked Caitlin. She shook her head, as though she was trying to let it all sink in.

'A few minutes later,' Gez said, finishing his story,

'you two were there, with some woman. And it was all over.'

'No,' Caitlin said with certainty. 'It isn't all over. Someone hurt my dad. We have to find out what's going on.'

Ali looked at Caitlin. She looked stern, with her eyebrows set in a frown. The log he was sitting on felt damp and cold. He wriggled uncomfortably. He had enjoyed pretending to investigate, but now they knew what Gez had seen, he felt a bit different.

'Caitlin,' he said slowly, 'you were right. There is something odd going on. A gang doing something secret. But this is grown-up stuff. Should we really chase them? Perhaps now we should just let Dave go to the police. They'll catch them.'

Caitlin shook her head impatiently, 'Dad won't do that.'

'He won't go to the police? Why not?'

Gez laughed.

Ali didn't see what was funny. 'No, really. Why not? If someone hurt him, then the police will help. Look at the crime scene, get DNA samples, stuff like that. They'd catch them, easy.'

Gez shook his head. 'I can tell you're new. Caitlin's dad can't go to the cops. They'd arrest him soon as look at him. He's a gangster.'

'You take that back!' Caitlin said angrily.

'What?' Gez asked. 'I was only saying what everyone knows. I wasn't being mean – honest, Caitlin.'

'My dad is *not* a criminal. He's a businessman.'

'All right,' Gez said, holding his hands up, 'he's a businessman. Whatever you say.'

'So why can't he go to the police then?' Ali asked.

Caitlin frowned harder. 'Ali, Dad's business is looking after other people's dogs. At the top of a tower block. In a rented flat. What do you think would happen if the police came round?'

Oh. Ali suddenly felt a bit dense. He hadn't known that what Dave was doing wasn't allowed. Dave'd be in big trouble if anyone found out; he might even lose the flat. So there would be no police. 'OK, fine. Sorry. But what can we do about it? We can't do DNA tests.'

Caitlin stood up, knocking the crate over as she did. 'We don't need DNA, we just need to investigate. Come on!' She walked away, through the bushes, back towards the path.

Ali looked at Gez. Gez grinned, then followed Caitlin. Ali shrugged; the mystery would be solved much quicker if they went to the police. But if they couldn't do that, then he would help his new friend find out who'd hurt her dad. He picked up Falcon's lead and led her out to hunt for clues.

Caitlin was already at the path when Ali and Falcon reached her.

'Gez,' she said, 'did the man come from this path? Or from somewhere else?'

Gez thought for a moment. 'He came from here. He was carrying something. He was waiting for his accomplice in the van when your dad turned up.'

'So,' Caitlin said, 'he must have come from the river. Let's go.'

They followed the path carefully, each step placed on clear ground for fear of destroying evidence. The path dropped steeply; Ali had to grab hold of tree branches to stop Falcon from pulling him over. The sound of the river got louder, water rushing over rocks. Ali had never been here before. The sight of the river when they finally reached it was a surprise. It was really wide! From the top of Lever Tower it had looked narrow, but it wasn't; the shallow water at the edge gave way to deep, black water in the centre. The far bank was thirty metres or more away.

'Wow! It's a proper river,' he said.

'What were you expecting? It goes out to the sea just a mile or two away,' Caitlin said.

Ali walked to the edge of the bank and looked in. The water ran over pebbles and tiny dark fish darted in tight formations. 'Fish and everything!' he said.

Gez came up close to him and peered in too. 'Yes. Too small for fishing though. We could put some in a jam jar and take them back to the den. We could have an aquarium like in a Chinese restaurant.'

'Hey!' Caitlin yelled. 'Will you two stop messing about? We are looking for evidence. Leave those poor fish be.'

Ali sighed and turned away. With Falcon at his side, he inspected the ground, looking for any sign of the man who had been here the night before. 'There's a plastic bag here. And another one. But they're all scrunched up, they look old,' he said.

'And some old beer cans here. And some cigarette ends,' Gez said from further along the bank.

'Do you think we should take the cigarette ends? On the telly, they can tell who's the criminal by what brand they smoke,' Caitlin said doubtfully.

'There's no way I'm collecting piles of dirty old fag ends. If they're clues, then you'll just have to work it out without them,' Gez said.

Ali looked at the ground carefully. The path led straight to the water and a kind of small, stony beach. On either side of the path, the grass was undisturbed.

'Hey!' he said. The others turned to look at him. 'The path is all muddy. But the grass hasn't been trampled!'

Gez shrugged. Caitlin frowned.

Ali sighed. 'That means that the man didn't walk on the grass last night. Which means that the only place he could have come from is the river. He must have come by boat!' He grinned. Perhaps this investigating business would be easy after all. 'So he unloaded something from his boat into the van, and Dave saw him do it.'

'I wonder what was in the box?' Caitlin asked. 'It must be something secret. Why else would they do it at night?'

Gez shook his head. 'Dunno. Could've been anything! Drugs! Guns! Ancient artefacts! Priceless paintings!'

'And your dad really won't tell us what he saw?' Ali asked.

'No,' Caitlin said. 'He won't say anything.'

'Well, in that case, there's only one way to find out,' Gez said.

'What way's that?' Ali asked.

'Stake-out,' Gez said.

CHAPTER 5

'Stake-out?' Ali asked. 'You mean we should come here tonight and spy?'

'Yup,' Gez said. 'We could find out what's in the boxes.'

'Cool.'

Ali's stomach rumbled loudly; it was time to eat. Mum would make thick-cut tuna sandwiches for lunch, if he asked nicely. 'I have to go home,' he said. 'But I can meet you both here tonight, maybe at eight o'clock?'

Caitlin shook her head. 'There's no way Dad will let me out at that time. Not after last night. You two go, and make sure you tell me exactly what goes on. I've not got a mobile, but you have to ring the flat as soon as you have news, OK?'

Ali took out his phone. 'What's your number? Gez,

yours too.' They told him and he keyed them in. 'Excellent. I'll see you back here tonight.'

A few minutes later, he let himself into the flat. It was beginning to feel like home already.

'Mum?'

'There you are!' Mum came out of her bedroom.

'Mum, what are you doing?' Ali stared. Mum was wearing the red minidress that she'd found yesterday. It was tiny. And she wore huge boots, with thick soles. It looked like she had bricks strapped to her feet.

Mum twirled slowly – it was clearly tricky to do in the boots. 'Do you like it? This was my Spice Girls outfit. I don't suppose you remember them. I used to go out in this! I was wearing it the first time I met your dad. And he still asked me out!'

'It looks, er, nice.'

'Oh, you are a good boy. I can't believe I can still get into it. There's loads of stuff I'd completely forgotten about. Some of your stuff too. I should have given it to a charity shop ages ago.'

'No!' Ali said. He thought about the things in boxes, the things that Dad would have recognised.

'What?' Mum asked.

Ali shook his head. He hadn't meant to shout. But

the idea of throwing their things away gave him a strange feeling, like an ache in the middle of his chest. Mum was standing closer now. She cupped his chin in her hand.

'What is it, sweetheart?' she asked gently.

'Nothing.' He pulled back.

'Come and have a look.' Mum sounded excited. She went into her room. Ali followed, not sure why he didn't want to. But he was sure that he didn't.

Mum's bedroom looked like an explosion at a jumble sale. Half-empty boxes spilled clothes and toys on to the floor. There were piles of fabric on the bed, red, gold, pink; things that Mum had already tried on.

Something blue caught Ali's eye. A man's T-shirt, twisted around an old toy truck. He lifted it gently from the box. It smelled of dust and old places. It didn't smell like Dad any more.

'Oh, Ali,' Mum said softly.

'It's OK,' Ali said, trying his best to mean it. He paused. 'Do you . . . Do you think he might come back soon?' Even as he said the words, he wished he hadn't. Mum didn't want Dad back. Ali knew that. She remembered the rows, the arguing, the slammed doors and angry words. And Ali remembered them too.

But he also remembered the way it felt to have Dad hold him tight and whisper goodnight. It was like being held by a rock, or an oak tree. Solid and for ever.

He twisted the T-shirt around his fingers.

'I don't know,' Mum said finally. 'I don't think so. But then, I've never known what goes on in your dad's head. He might come back one day.'

Ali dropped the T-shirt back into the box.

Mum pulled off the boots. 'So, where have you been this morning?' she asked.

'I went to see Caitlin. I left you a note.'

'I know. But I went to their flat . . .' Mum paused. 'Dave said he hadn't seen you.'

'He was asleep. Caitlin and me, we went out,' Ali shrugged.

Mum tugged on a pair of jeans. Then she pulled a jumper over the dress. The bottom of it still showed, like a sparkly red belt.

'Ali,' she said. Her voice was serious. 'We're making a new start here. Both of us. Without your dad.'

'I know.'

'Do you? Life goes on, you know. I need to start living again.'

Ali nodded, though he wasn't really sure what she meant.

'It's been lonely for me too. I'm not saying I want your dad back; we were bad for each other. But I do miss the company.'

Mum was lonely? Ali looked down at his lap. He hadn't known that. He thought it was just him that missed Dad. 'But you won't be lonely here, will you? You've got me,' he said.

She smiled at him in an odd way. 'Yes, I've got you. And I'm sure I'll make new friends. You wouldn't mind that, would you?'

'Of course not.'

'Good.' Mum patted his shoulder quickly.

Ali nodded, but couldn't think of anything to say.

'Come on. This flat looks like a bomb's hit it. We need to spend the day getting it shipshape.'

'I was going to go out again, later,' Ali said.

'But you've been out all morning! I thought we could get all this done, then I'll cook something nice for tea and then we'll watch a film from under our duvets. Just you and me. What do you say?'

He had to say yes. He couldn't let Mum feel lonely. Gez would have to do the stake-out on his own.

CHAPTER 6

wht cn u c? Ali hit send and settled back on to his bed.

Moments later, his mobile bleeped. It was a reply from Gez. *Nothing. Still. Stop txting me. I'll call u.*

Ali's phone rang. This time it was Caitlin. 'Gez just told me to stop ringing him. It's not fair. Just because I haven't got a mobile and can't text. He says I'm bothering him.' Caitlin sounded cross.

Ali grinned. No wonder Gez was annoyed if they were both getting in touch every two minutes. And it wasn't even night-time yet. 'Don't worry,' he told Caitlin. 'I'll let you know if anything happens. He told me to stop fussing too.'

'I can't help it.'

Ali chuckled. 'Sorry, Caitlin, you'll have to try.' He finished the call.

Ali looked out of his bedroom window. The sky was

turning dark and low mist was forming. The lights of the town seemed far away.

In the kitchen, Mum was frying onions. The smell made him hungry. He left his phone on the windowsill and went through to see her.

'Smells good,' he said. He opened the bread bin and looked inside.

'Don't even think about it. Tea's ready in ten minutes,' Mum said. 'Make yourself useful and get a couple of plates, will you?'

Ali had unpacked the kitchen stuff that afternoon, so he knew where the plates were. He found the salt and pepper and put those on the table too.

'Do you think I should have asked Dave and Caitlin to eat with us?' Mum asked.

'What? Why?'

'Oh, you know. Because he got hurt. He might not feel like cooking tonight. He still looked poorly when I called there this morning. Well, it's too late now, anyway. I haven't cooked enough. But perhaps I should take them something tomorrow?'

'If you want,' Ali said, though he was sure that Dave didn't need Mum cooking for him.

His phone rang. He could hear it coming from the bedroom. Mum rolled her eyes at him. 'Whoever it is, tell them you'll call back. Tea's nearly ready.'

Ali raced to his room. Perhaps Gez had some news already! He made it just before the ring tone chimed its last few notes. The screen said it was Caitlin again.

'Hello,' Ali said.

'Anything happening?'

'No. It's only teatime.'

'I know, but it's driving me mental. I know you boys will forget to ring me. You'll forget and go off investigating and you won't even notice I'm not there. At least, you won't until some bad men capture you and you think, *Oh, wouldn't it have been good to tell Caitlin cos then she'd know where we are and come and rescue us, but instead we're going to be trapped in this dungeon for ever and ever.*'

'Caitlin. How can I forget when you're calling me every two minutes?'

'You just will, I know it. Listen, can I come and wait at yours?'

'What, now?'

'Yes. Ask your mum if you can have a sleepover. That way I'll be there whenever Gez gets in touch.'

'What?'

'A sleepover. You know, when someone sleeps over?'

'Oh, I see. I'll have to ask Mum. Wait there.'

Ali held the phone tight to him, so that all Caitlin would hear was the scratching of his jumper on the speaker. Then he went back to the kitchen. 'Mum, can Caitlin come and stay at ours tonight?'

'Caitlin?'

'Yes. She, er, she's going to tell me about the school and the teachers and stuff. So that I'm ready for after the holidays.'

Mum smiled slightly. 'Yes, if you like. Tell her to bring a sleeping bag or something. She'll have to sleep on cushions on your floor.'

That was a yes! Without even saying anything embarrassing about Caitlin being his *girlfriend* in a soppy Mum voice. Ali lifted his phone again. 'Bring a sleeping bag. You'll have to sleep on cushions.'

'OK, I'll be there in fifteen minutes.' She hung up.

Ali looked at his phone. He had a friend coming to stay in fifteen minutes. He'd only been here two days and he'd made friends. Two of them. He grinned widely. Then something occurred to him. It wasn't *him* she was coming to visit, it was his *mobile*. She wanted information from Gez and it was quicker to come here to get it. She wasn't visiting a friend, she was visiting a phone.

He sat down heavily. Mum had put the food out already. He picked up his fork and shovelled some up to his mouth.

'What's the matter?' Mum asked.

'Nothing.'

Mum smiled at him and patted his shoulder. 'It's probably just nerves. Don't fret – I'm sure you'll have fun.'

Caitlin arrived after dinner. Ali washed up and then showed her his room. He was pleased that Mum had made him unpack properly. His room was looking good. He had his books on the shelf, his clothes put away and some posters on the walls: a lion, a polar bear and one of Jason Adams in his Liverpool strip taking a shot at goal.

Caitlin arranged her Bratz sleeping bag and the sofa cushions on the floor. 'You like animals,' she said.

'Yes. I want to be a vet when I grow up.'

She looked at the books on his shelf. 'This one's falling apart.' She pulled out the *Giant Atlas of World Animals*. It was true that the spine was hanging loose.

'Careful,' Ali said. 'Dad gave me that.'

Caitlin slipped the book back on to the shelf and turned to look at him. 'So,' she said, 'where is your dad?'

Ali froze. That wasn't the sort of question you asked if you were visiting a phone. That was a personal, private question.

'Ali?' Caitlin asked again.

Ali caught his breath. Just for a second he saw flashing blue eyes, all crinkled at the corners with a smile. Dad.

After a few moments of silence, Caitlin spoke again. 'Did he die, like my mum?'

Caitlin's mum was dead? Ali tried to remember whether she or Gez had told him that. How had he not known?

'Ali?' Caitlin said. 'You don't have to tell me if you don't want to.'

'Oh,' Ali said quickly, 'no, he's not dead. Nothing like that. He's in Asia. India, probably.'

'India? But you said he was from Scotland. You said you were hardly Indian at all. You said –'

Ali took the book from Caitlin. 'I know what I said,' Ali began. 'And it's true. Dad is from Scotland. He married my mum and then they had me. And I think that's when the trouble started. They didn't have much money. Dad didn't really have much of a job. He played dhol.'

'He played with dolls?' Caitlin sounded horrified.

Ali grinned. 'No, dhol. It's a kind of drum. He played it at weddings and things. Mum liked it at first. But then, they rowed.'

'Why?' Caitlin sat down on the cushions and curled the sleeping bag around herself.

'I think I cost too much. When I was little, Mum wanted Dad to get a proper job, so that they could buy all the things they needed. I remember listening from upstairs, when they thought I was asleep. It would start with them talking about the price of a school trip and end with the two of them yelling their heads off. I used to hold a pillow over my head, so that I didn't have to listen.'

'Then what happened?'

Ali shrugged. 'One day, Dad just left. He said he was a musician, not a doormat. He went to India to learn. He sends postcards sometimes. He's travelled all over. I think . . .' Ali's voice dropped to a whisper. 'I think he's glad to be away from us.'

'Do you miss him?'

Ali couldn't speak. His eyes felt too hot. He looked away, so that Caitlin couldn't see.

'Sorry,' Caitlin said.

'It's OK. We're making a new start, Mum says.'

'I like your mum,' Caitlin said. She paused. 'Dad does too. He thinks it was nice of her to come and look for him last night.'

Ali frowned.

'And she's really pretty,' Caitlin said. 'She looks like the ladies in shampoo adverts. Exotic.'

Exotic? Mum? Ali screwed up his face. Mum wasn't

exotic. Her favourite meal was bangers and mash. She never missed an episode of *EastEnders*.

'She's not exotic,' he said finally.

Caitlin sat up and stared at him. 'Ali! She is so! She's got beautiful dark hair, like . . . like silk. And big brown eyes that look almost black. And her skin is like peaches. She's lovely! She's like an Asian princess . . . like Pocahontas.'

'Pocahontas was American!' Ali snapped. Was that how people saw Mum? The idea made him feel uncomfortable. She wasn't exotic, she was just Mum.

There was a pause.

'Sorry,' Caitlin said. 'I was only saying. She's pretty, that's all. It's a compliment.'

Ali didn't reply. Caitlin sighed.

'What time is it?' Caitlin asked.

Ali looked at his clock. 'Nearly ten.'

'It was about this time last night that Dad went out. Gez might ring soon. Do you think he'll find out anything?'

'I hope so. It would be good, wouldn't it? To be detectives. To solve a mystery.'

Caitlin was quiet, then she said, 'I don't care much about the mystery. I just want to find out who hurt my dad.'

They lay still for a moment. The only sound in the

room was the ticking of Ali's alarm clock.

Then his phone rang. Caitlin dived towards the bedside table, but Ali got there first. Gez. Ali pressed loudspeaker, so that Caitlin could hear.

'Gez? What's going on?'

'I have eyeball,' Gez said, his voice crackly over the speaker.

'You what?' Caitlin asked.

'Is that Caitlin? What are you doing there?'

'Sleepover,' Ali said quickly. 'What can you see?'

'I have eyeball on the suspect,' Gez said proudly.

'You mean you can see him?' Caitlin said.

'Yes. Yes, I can, OK. Blimey, Caitlin, where's your sense of adventure?'

'Stop rabbiting on and tell us what you can see!' Caitlin said.

'OK. Picture the scene. It's dark. I'm at my window, looking out. I hear an owl hoot down in the blackness.'

'The man, Gez! The man!' Caitlin said.

'Fine, fine. Look, there's a white van. It just got here. It's parked in the lane. There's only one person in it, a driver. No one else. It's just waiting.'

'Anything written on it? Any markings?' Ali asked.

'Negative. At least, I think negative. To be honest, it's a bit too dark to tell. I could sneak out for a closer look.'

'No,' Ali said immediately. 'It's too dangerous.'

Caitlin frowned. 'It's our only lead. I know this gang is dangerous, but the driver won't suspect a boy. And he might not even see Gez. He was pretty good at stalking us, remember?'

'Yes,' Gez said. 'I'll be like his shadow. He won't know I'm there. We need a lead, else we have nothing.'

Ali sat still on his bed. Caitlin was looking at him, waiting for his decision. Since when was he in charge? Ali felt a sudden shiver; Caitlin and Gez really did think that he was the leader! How had that happened? They barely knew him. He swallowed slowly. 'You're right,' he said. 'This is our best lead. Gez, here's what you do. You sneak out into your yard. If you have a cat or something, take that with you. The driver'll think you're just letting the cat out. Take a quick look. *Don't* get close. *Don't* speak to him. Then come straight inside and phone us. Be careful! Understood?'

'Roger that. Like a shadow, but one that can make phone calls. Over and out.'

CHAPTER 7

Gez closed his phone with a sharp snap.

His mission was clear. He had to get an identification on the men. He had to do it secretly. And if he could find out what was in the boxes, then all the better.

It was a good job that he was feeling like a superhero tonight. But then, there were few nights when he didn't feel like a superhero.

He put the phone down on his brother's bedside table. It was Michael's phone after all. Percy, the grass snake that Michael kept in an old aquarium, hissed gently. Was it a warning? An omen?

'Shh!' Gez said to Percy.

The window was open. Michael always left it ajar in case he missed curfew and had to climb in late. But tonight it was Gez breaking the rules. He needed a cover story. He needed to be able to explain what he was doing outside, in case anyone saw him. He didn't have a cat to put out – his mum was allergic. But he had left his bike outside, thrown down in the yard just under the washing line in the way that drove Mum insane.

That would do! He would pretend to be just a regular little boy, bringing in his abandoned bike before bedtime. Genius!

Gez eased open the window. The sudden rush of cold air made him shiver. He climbed over the window-sill and dropped gently on to the kitchen roof. He steadied himself on the tiles. Then, with a quick scurry, he was across the roof and above the lawn. He lowered himself over the edge, trying not to scrape his belly on the gutter. Then, lightly, he landed on the ground. Excellent. He would get to the bottom of this mystery tonight.

He suddenly realised that it was freezing outside. Why hadn't he thought to put his coat on? What if he got kidnapped in just his Spiderman pyjamas? He did a few quick star jumps to get warm, then left the garden.

The back lane was deserted – black and bare as a tomb.

Apart from the van.

It was parked about thirty metres away. He would have to creep up on it, take the driver by surprise. He inched closer. The number plate was covered in mud, hiding the letters. *Cunning*, Gez thought.

He was getting closer, closer . . .

He could see the side now. There was nothing there. No, name, or picture. No, wait! There was something! Gez crouched down and scurried nearer. There were raised patches on the paintwork. Something had been *painted over*. It was just about possible to read the old name – Tones and Sons. Brilliant! This mission was a doddle.

Then a phone rang. Inside the van.

'Yes?' a man's voice said.

Gez froze.

He knew he should run. Knew he should get home, get safe, call Ali with the name he'd found. But his legs wouldn't listen. They inched closer to the van door, so that he could hear better.

'Of course I'm ready,' the man said. 'Tonight? Sure, why not?' There was a pause. 'That bird still giving you trouble? Don't worry. I'll take care of her. She'll be gone by Sunday. Trust me, you won't hear a squeak from her ever again.'

Gez's legs turned to jelly. What was wrong with his legs tonight? Perhaps they didn't like hearing murder threats. He couldn't blame them. He had to get out of here. *Now.*

An owl hooted by the river. *Tu-whit-tu.*

Whoo, the reply came. From the driver's seat in the van!

From the van?

Gez looked from the van to the river, then back again. The driver had made the noise. The gang were using the hoots to communicate. There were no owls. There never had been. He felt disappointed. He'd been listening to them for weeks. Well, at least the foxes were real, even if they had gone missing.

'Oi!' a voice bellowed, just behind him.

Gez turned slowly. Two men hurried towards him. Their dark shapes seemed huge in the starlight. One of them was carrying an awkward-shaped bundle.

'Oi! You! What you doing by our van?'

A few paces away, Gez heard a metallic click: the van door opening. The driver got out. Gez was caught between them. He was sandwiched. He was toast. He was a toasted sandwich.

Suddenly, his legs sprang into action, he dodged forwards, sidestepping left, then right. The men tried to step with him, but they couldn't keep up. Gez turned and darted into the woods. He crashed through the first bush. Twigs and thorns tore at his face, but he carried on, diving down into the thick cover of night.

'Where did he go?' one of the men shouted. The voice wasn't far away. Gez froze, desperate not to give away his hiding place.

'Can't have gone far. Want me to look for him, Woody?'

There was silence.

'No,' Woody said eventually. 'It was just some kid. No need to worry.'

'Do you think he saw anything?'

'What could he have seen?'

'I dunno. Nothing. We just can't take chances. Not after last night.'

There was a cold laugh. 'I heard there was trouble. The boss was angry?'

'Yes. O'Connor was on the warpath.'

'So I heard,' Woody said. 'Come on, or we'll be next.'

Gez held his breath, struggling not to gasp. O'Connor! That was Caitlin's surname! Were they talking about Caitlin? No, she didn't know anything. It had to be her dad. Why would he be on the warpath?

Unless.

Gez felt shivers run up his spine. He had heard the rumours about Caitlin's dad being dodgy, everyone had. And this gang sounded scared of him. What if he was angry with them because he was the one in charge?

No, that didn't make sense. They had attacked him last night. They wouldn't attack their own boss.

Unless they'd had an argument. A mutiny.

And now they were worrying about what O'Connor would do for revenge.

Gez shuddered. He had to get back to his bedroom safely and call Ali.

He was near to the den. Gez knew this little patch of wood like it was his own home. He edged backwards, slow, real slow. There was a low branch just behind him. He stepped over it neatly, treading gently on the wet fallen leaves. He kept his eyes forward; the pale shape of the van was still just in view. He needed to get round it somehow. If he kept creeping back and right, he would trace a big arc around the men and find himself back on the road. He could slip right past them to the front of his own home.

He moved, creeping slowly away from the van. It was out of sight now, and so were the men. The starlight was shrouded by clouds. It was very dark. Were the men still on the road? Gez strained to listen, but all he could hear were the strange scurries and shuffles of other creatures out in the woods. Or was it footsteps? Had Woody been bluffing? Were the gang looking for him after all?

CHAPTER 8

'He's been gone for ages,' Caitlin said.

Ali squirmed under his duvet. She was right – it had been too long.

'Do you think he's OK?' she asked.

'Course he is. What could happen to him?'

'Oh, you know, he could get beaten up, or kidnapped, or he could have just tripped over and broken his leg and now he's lying outside in the freezing cold, shivering to death cos no one but us knows where he is.'

Ali didn't answer.

Caitlin sat up, pushing back her sleeping bag. 'We have to do something, I can't stand this.'

'What can we do? My mum would freak if we sneaked out, and we can't tell her that we're going, cos she'd double-freak.' Ali looked across. In the glow from his night light Caitlin looked cross and crumpled. He was beginning to realise that when she looked cross it really meant that she was worried. 'I'm sure he'll be OK, you know. He's not stupid.'

Caitlin snorted. 'You've only known him for a day! I promise you, they don't come any stupider than Gez Brown.'

'So what do you think we should do?'

She sighed and lay back down. 'I don't know. I just wish he would ring.'

'Me too.'

The phone rang. Ali leapt up and grabbed it from his bedside table. 'It's him!' He pressed it to his ear. 'Hello? Where have you been?' Ali listened for a moment, then frowned. 'But are you OK? I told you to be careful!' More listening, more frowning. Ali looked at Caitlin. She wasn't going to like this, not at all. He put the phone down slowly.

'Well?' Caitlin said eagerly.

'He saw three men. One of them was called Woody.' Ali looked at her face, trying to tell whether she recognised the name. She didn't seem to.

'And?'

'He saw the van, and other stuff. He wants to meet up tomorrow to tell us all about it. He nearly got caught.'

'No!' Caitlin pulled her knees up and hugged them inside her sleeping bag. 'What else did he say?'

Ali shrugged.

'Ali! Tell me.'

He sighed. 'Gez heard them say "O'Connor".'

Caitlin shrugged. 'Well, they would, wouldn't they? They beat Dad up right in that spot, just last night. They would be thinking about it.'

Ali twisted the edge of his duvet into a little ball. 'It might be more than that. Gez said they seemed scared of him.'

Caitlin grinned. 'They should be more scared of us! We're getting close to them, aren't we? We just need to find out what they've got in the boxes. I bet it's stolen jewels. You know, crowns and things.' She settled back on to her cushions and closed her eyes.

Ali was sure that she would dream of queens and palaces and balls tonight. He had done a really bad job of explaining what Gez had heard. She hadn't even seemed to hear what he'd said. But he had to admit to himself that he hadn't tried very hard. He didn't want to upset her. Dave was all she'd got. He sighed. This was getting more difficult by the minute.

CHAPTER 9

'Orange juice and toast all round!' Mum said.

Ali sat at the breakfast table.

Caitlin sat next to him and smiled warmly. 'Thanks, Mrs Ferguson.'

'Yuck. Don't call me that. I haven't been that in years. Call me Anita,' Mum said.

'OK . . . Anita.' Caitlin turned pink.

Ali spread a thick layer of jam over his toast and took a huge bite. Caitlin wasn't being prickly or grumpy this morning. She was . . . he thought for a moment; she was *happy*. She seemed to have forgotten all about what Gez had overheard. Could Dave really be part of the gang? He took another bite of his toast.

'What will you do today?' Mum asked.

He shrugged.

'I have to get home to walk Falcon,' Caitlin said.

'Ali, do you want to come?'

Ali shook his head. He needed time to think. If Dave was part of the gang, then that changed everything. He watched silently as Caitlin left the flat.

CHAPTER 10

Caitlin hummed a tune as she walked to her front door. She shimmied and twirled right around before putting her key in the lock.

'Ta-da!' she said. 'I'm home!' She dropped her sleeping bag on the hall table. Falcon hurtled towards her, her tail wagging like windscreen wipers in a downpour. 'Hello, Falcon, hello. Have you been looking after Dad?' Caitlin said, ruffling her hands through the dog's warm fur. 'Good girl.'

'Caitlin? Is that you?' Dad asked.

'Who else would it be? Did you miss me?' Caitlin waltzed through into the living room. 'No, don't tell me, you'll only embarrass yourself.'

'Charming.' Dad laughed. He was sat on the sofa, still in his dressing gown. He put his coffee down on the table. 'Did you have a good time?'

Caitlin dropped down next to him and snuggled into his hug. 'Yup!' He hadn't shaved yet and the stubble on his chin felt rough against her forehead. She pulled away. 'Ow, you're scratchy.'

'Sorry.'

'I think,' Caitlin said, 'that Ali's mum is *lovely*.'

Dad turned a bit pink.

I knew it! thought Caitlin

'I think you should mind your own business.' Dad grinned.

'What did I say? I didn't say anything. Anita is nice, that's all. I was just stating a fact.'

Dad stood up. 'I'm going to get showered. It was peaceful here before you came home. Wasn't it, Falcon?'

Caitlin felt a little fizz of excitement. If Dad was avoiding her, then he must like Anita! 'I'm going to take Falcon for a walk, OK?'

Dad frowned. 'Perhaps I'd better come with you.'

'Why? You're not even dressed yet.'

'I know. But you shouldn't go out by yourself.'

The fizz inside Caitlin died down a little. Why was Dad worried about her going out with Falcon? They went out together all the time.

'What's going on?' she asked.

'Just after the other night . . .' Dad said.

'What? What about it? Is there something I should know?' Caitlin said.

'No, no. Nothing. It doesn't matter.' Dad shrugged, then said, 'You're right. But be careful, OK?'

'Sure.'

'If you see anyone hanging around or anything, you come home.'

'Sure.'

Outside, the fizz came back. The sky was blue as sapphire and cloudless. Caitlin ran down the steps and on to the grass, with Falcon bounding at her side. Caitlin laughed aloud; she felt like a kite at the end of its string, soaring into the air. It would be so lovely if Dad got together with Anita.

Suddenly, Falcon slowed, her nose to the ground. Her head swung from left to right. She had smelled something interesting. For a few seconds, she sniffed. Then she was away again, speeding over the grass towards the road. The lead was taut between them as Caitlin sprinted to keep up. Falcon was hunting something.

Caitlin looked up.

A white van was parked by the kerb.

Falcon was heading straight towards it.

The side door of the van slid open, revealing the

dark space inside. Caitlin pulled Falcon's lead, desperate to stop her. But Falcon was too strong.

She was pulling them both towards the open door.

'Falcon! Stop!' Caitlin yelled. The lead bit into her hands, but still Falcon pulled her forward.

The van was just twenty metres away.

Fifteen metres.

Ten.

Falcon was headed straight for it.

'Falcon! No!'

There was a sudden movement in the doorway. A flash of bright orange fabric, waved like a flag. Falcon charged nearer.

Caitlin gripped the lead with both hands and jammed her feet down. She skidded over the grass, then fell. The lead twisted into her skin. Pain seared her wrist and jolted down her side, where she landed. She screamed with the shock of it.

Falcon stopped running.

Somewhere up ahead, she heard the van door slam and an engine start. The white van squealed away.

She lay still on the ground, winded. Falcon panted over her in concern.

'Falcon!' Caitlin sat up. 'What were you doing? Haven't you heard us talking about that van?'

Falcon whined gently.

Caitlin glanced at the road. The van turned the corner and was out of sight. What had just happened? Why was the van back? And at this time of day? She stood up slowly. Her hands were shaking. Dad was right; it wasn't safe out here alone. She realised that there were tears on her cheeks. She needed to find Gez and Ali fast. They had to find out what was going on.

CHAPTER 11

'I've made a CSI kit,' Gez said. He was sitting on the log in his den. He had a small suitcase open on one of the crates.

'A what?' Ali asked, pushing aside a branch as he walked in.

'A CSI kit. It's Mum's make-up case really. But she won't mind. I took her talc and one of her face brush-things, so that we can take fingerprints. And a notebook. And I've got food bags for collecting evidence.'

'Evidence?'

'Yup. There must be tons of evidence round here. If the gang keep coming back. Put your mobile in.'

'Why?'

'Because CSI always have radios in their kits. Go on.'

Ali grinned, then dropped his mobile in the case next to the talc. 'OK, PC Brown, let's go over the facts. Tell me again what happened last night.'

'I'm not a PC, I'm a detective inspector. And you're Detective Superintendent Ferguson.'

'Sorry, DI Brown. Please continue with your statement.'

'Well, I saw the van. And two suspects carrying an unknown item. But then they saw me!'

'No!'

'Yup. But I was too quick for them. I was like a cheetah, straight into the woods. And they fired guns after me.'

'No way!'

'Well, maybe not *guns*. It might have just been shouting. Anyway, I had to dive for cover.'

'They chased you?'

'For hours. But I went to ground. In a secret hiding place that only I know. And then I heard them talking. They were talking about Caitlin's dad. They sounded really *scared* of him. Like their mutiny had gone bad and they knew he was going to get back at them.'

'They said he was the boss?'

'Well, maybe not in those words exactly. But that was what they meant.'

Ali shivered. And not because of the cold. If Dave

was their prime suspect, it was bad news.

'Did you tell Caitlin what I heard? What did she say?' Gez asked.

'She didn't believe me. No, it was like she didn't even hear me. Gez, what were they bringing onshore? Did you get a look at it?'

Gez nodded. 'It was something funny-shaped.'

'Funny-shaped? Like what exactly?'

Gez shrugged. 'If I knew that, I'd have said, wouldn't I? It was a funny shape. Lumpy. And there were weird noises.'

'Funny *and* weird. DI Brown, that's the worst description I've ever heard.'

'Ha ha, very funny. Hey, I've got a notepad in the CSI kit. I'll draw it for you.' Gez rummaged for a minute, then pulled out a spiral-bound notebook, with a pencil pushed into the coil of wire. He sketched quickly, then held the picture up for Ali to see.

'Yes, funny and weird. You're right,' Ali said. Gez had drawn a blob, round at the top and square at the bottom. 'It looks a bit like a ghost.'

Gez laughed. 'Ghost smuggling! That's cool! Do you suppose they bring in headless knights and set them free in ruined castles? You know, for tourists? That's a brilliant idea!'

'OK, maybe not. What else did you see?'

'The name on the van. Painted out for secrecy – Tones and Sons.'

'Great! We can find out about that dead easy. We just need a phone book. Do you want to do that now?' Ali said.

'Sure. Let's go to mine, it's closer. And I'm starving.'

They got up. Gez carried the CSI kit. Ali followed him out through the brambles.

'Ali!' a voice shouted. Ali looked up. Caitlin was running towards them, Falcon at her side. 'Gez!' she yelled.

'Looks like she's cross again,' Gez said.

'Looks like something's happened,' said Ali. He ran to meet her. As he got closer, he could see the dried tear-tracks that stained her face. 'Caitlin, what is it? Is it your dad?'

Caitlin shook her head. 'No. The van. I saw it.'

'What, just now? In the daytime?'

Caitlin nodded. 'I've been looking for you. You weren't at home.' Tears glistened in her eyes.

'It's OK,' Ali said. 'It's OK now.'

'How is it? Someone just tried to kidnap Falcon. Or me. Or both of us!'

'What?' Ali said, horrified.

'Falcon ran straight to the van. They must have laid a trail. They had Miss Osborne's orange top. Falcon

72

followed it. And the door opened . . . and we were nearly inside, but I stopped Falcon just in time. They were after us, Ali!' Caitlin's face was white, and her voice shook.

This was bad. This was really bad. This didn't feel like a game any more.

'We'll find out who they are,' Ali told Caitlin in a voice much surer than he felt. 'We've got a name. We've got a lead. Come on.'

CHAPTER 12

Ali watched Gez run his finger down the page.

'There's nothing here,' Gez moaned. He was holding a huge phone book open on the kitchen table. The room was crowded. Gez's mum was unpacking shopping, her hair coming loose from its ponytail as she worked. Gez's older brothers, Owen and Michael, were busy tasting everything before she put it away. They were working as a team, one distracting their mum while the other swiped something.

'Give it here,' Caitlin said. She yanked the heavy book from Gez and flipped through a few pages. All the businesses in the area were listed alphabetically. But there was nothing under Tones.

'Who took the biscuits?' Gez's mum yelled.

'Perhaps they're not local?' Gez suggested.

Ali leaned in to look over Caitlin's shoulder. The

business names went straight from 'Tomas the Jewellers' to 'Toppers Gentlemen's Outfitters'.

'Tones sounds like a music shop. Or perhaps a paint shop?' Gez said.

'Or perhaps you read it wrong,' Caitlin said.

Ali closed the book in disgust. 'Dead end,' he said.

'Put those crisps away now! And leave that pop alone. Must you all be in here?' Gez's mum sounded harassed.

Ali smiled at her apologetically. Gez didn't seem to hear anything she yelled.

'We should just go and look for the white van,' Gez said. 'Search the town until we find it. Get all the kids we know to start looking.'

Caitlin shook her head. 'Like we'd ever find it. Would you even recognise the men again?'

'Enough!' Gez's mum said as Michael swiped a whole box of microwave chips. 'All of you. Out! Now!'

Ali thought for a minute. They couldn't just wander around hoping to stumble across a criminal gang. That only happened in stories. *But*, he thought, *we could retrace their steps.*

'Am I talking to myself?' Gez's mum yelled.

'We should go along the river,' Ali said. 'To the docks. To see where they came from. And we should get out of your mum's way.'

'Is this my make-up case?' Gez's mum shouted as she picked up the CSI kit.

Gez chuckled. 'She loves this really. Don't pay any attention.'

'OUT!'

Gez jumped. 'Yes,' he said quickly, 'OK. Let's check out the river.'

CHAPTER 13

They fought their way through the brambles and drifts of litter that lined the banks of the river. The water swelled to their right. To their left, warehouses crouched among the thin strip of woodland.

'Not far,' Gez said. 'Just a mile, I think.'

'Yuck.' Caitlin shook an old lolly wrapper off her foot.

The river was held in check by concrete banks. Ali noticed that as they walked, the banks spread further apart. Water, banks, sky were all the same shade of hundred-wash grey. They were at the port.

And there was the sea!

It moved in swirls of navy and black, like a giant snake shedding its skin. A few fishing boats bobbed near the port wall. Further out, much further, huge cargo ships patrolled the depths.

'Caitlin,' Ali said, 'I've been thinking. How did the gang get hold of Miss Osborne's top? The orange one.'

Caitlin stopped walking and turned to Ali. Her face looked pale. 'I don't know. Perhaps they broke into her house and took it.'

'Oh no!' Gez gasped.

'What?'

'I just remembered something. Something Woody said last night! I can't believe I forgot it!'

'Well, spit it out,' Caitlin said crossly.

'He said they had a woman. One who was being difficult. But that they would get rid of her on Sunday!'

'What?'

'I know. I'm sorry. I'm a rubbish detective inspector. It just went out of my head,' Gez mumbled.

Ali stepped closer and put a hand on Gez's shoulder. 'It's OK. Tell us exactly what you heard.'

'Just that they had a woman, and she wouldn't be making trouble after Sunday. It was a threat.'

'Murder?' Ali felt cold.

Gez nodded slowly.

'That's it. I've had enough,' Caitlin said. She turned away from the port and started pushing back through the undergrowth.

'Where are you going?' Ali asked.

'To find Miss Osborne. To stop these people!'

'Caitlin. That's exactly what we are doing right now. Following the clues. Come on – you can't just rush off, you don't know where to start looking. The docks are our main lead right now.'

'But these people might be murderers. And they're after my dad!'

'But,' Gez said, 'your dad is –'

'Safe and sound at home!' Ali interrupted.

Ali tried to glare at Gez without Caitlin noticing. Gez had been about to say Dave was the boss! Ali shook his head. There was no way that Caitlin would believe that without proof. 'Come on,' he said. 'Keep your eyes open. We need to work out where they're coming from. And what they're bringing in that would be worth killing someone for.'

He pointed to a footbridge that led over the final stretch of river to the quay buildings on the other side. The bridge was rusty with age. Ali hoped it was still safe. He led them across it, treading carefully.

'My mum says this used to be a big, important port once,' Gez said, swinging down the last few steps of the bridge. 'Ships came from all over the world – America, India, Australia, you name it. Everyone came here. Not like now. I suppose they all use planes now.'

'Shh,' Caitlin said. 'You're meant to be looking, not talking.'

'Fine,' Gez said, and marched off ahead.

In a few moments, he rushed back. 'Suspect! Suspect in sight!'

'What?' Ali asked. 'Who?'

'Look!' Gez pointed downwards. Below the quay wall, a small fishing boat was moored to a huge iron ring. A man lay in the bottom of the boat, a hat covering his face. He wasn't moving.

'Is he asleep?' Ali whispered.

'Perhaps he's dead,' Gez said. 'Perhaps he's a victim, not a suspect.'

The man groaned and lifted the hat off his face. 'Perhaps he's just trying to get some rest,' he said.

Ali jumped back. Caitlin too.

'Let DI Brown handle this one,' Gez whispered. He stepped forward. 'Are you a fisherman? Do you work here?'

'Aye,' the man said. 'Here and all over. There aren't many places I haven't sailed.'

Gez's eyes lit up. 'Have you ever seen any sharks?' he asked.

The man grinned. 'One or two. Basking sharks round here.'

'What about octopus and giant squid?'

'Aye. I've seen some strange things at sea.'

'Like what?' Gez stepped forward eagerly.

The man sat up and reached for a cord that hung around his neck. He pulled it out; a tooth, pointed and fierce, hung from it. 'Here. I saw the shark that this came from. It was in Australia. It hunted along the Great Barrier Reef. It was the size of a bus, with teeth like razors.'

'Cool!' Gez grinned again.

The man shrugged. Then he tucked the tooth away again under his clothes.

Caitlin tutted. She stepped forward, pushing Gez out of the way. 'Do people still use the docks?' she asked. Ali snapped to attention. Caitlin was right: they were here to investigate and Gez was getting distracted.

'Of course. I'm here, aren't I?'

'Yes, but –'

'She means, is it still busy here?' Ali interrupted. 'Or would this be a good place to choose if you were doing something secret?'

'Secret?' The man frowned.

'Yes,' Gez said. 'You know, smuggling guns, or bringing in drugs. That sort of thing.'

'Smuggling? You've been watching too many films.'

'Doesn't it happen any more?' Caitlin asked.

'No. No, it doesn't,' the man said. 'And if it did, it isn't the sort of thing you should go asking about. You'll get yourselves into trouble. We might not have great white sharks here, but there are other dangerous things that travel these waters. Some nights, you can smell them in the air. You want to stay well clear.' The man stretched up and pulled the mooring rope free. He threw it down into the boat, without bothering to coil it. Then he pushed off the dock wall with the end of an oar.

The words *Deep Ocean* were painted in curly letters on the side. *On the hull,* Ali corrected himself. The *Deep Ocean* edged away from them. The man clearly wasn't going to tell them whatever it was he knew.

'What's the name of that boat?' Gez whispered. 'Seep? Qeep something?'

'It's Deep Ocean,' Ali said, surprised.

'I told you,' Caitlin said. 'He's not that bright.'

'That's not true!' Gez said sharply. 'I just can't read that silly swirly writing. It's stupid, not me!'

Caitlin was ready to answer. This was headed towards a proper row, Ali thought. And just because of some daft lettering.

Ali's eyes widened. He had thought of something. 'Gez,' he said, 'the writing on the van – did it look like this?' He drew quickly in the dust by their feet.

Jones

'Yeh,' Gez said slowly. 'It did a bit.'

Ali grinned. Even Caitlin smiled a bit.

'Gez,' Ali said, 'it isn't a "T", it's a "J". It's Jones and Sons.'

Gez's face fell. Ali couldn't stand to see him look so unhappy. 'Don't worry. It's an easy mistake to make, especially in the dark. Especially when it had been painted over.'

'And especially when the gangsters were chasing after me!' Gez said, more brightly.

'Exactly,' Ali said. 'At least now we know who we're looking for. Come on, let's get back to that phone book!'

CHAPTER 14

'There are a few Joneses. Hundreds, in fact,' Caitlin said, running her finger down the page. 'But only one Jones and Sons. And it's a pet shop! We've got them!'

She stood up.

'Where are you going?' Ali asked.

'To find the people who hurt my dad. And tried to take my dog. And kidnapped Miss Osborne!' Caitlin said.

'Caitlin, sit down,' Ali said firmly. To his amazement, Caitlin did. 'We can't just go rushing off there. It's getting dark. The shop's probably closed now anyway.'

Caitlin looked out of Gez's kitchen window. The sky was navy-black. The *EastEnders* theme tune started in the living room. 'OK,' she said. 'But first thing tomorrow – and I mean first thing, Gez – we go to that shop and we are going to find out what's going on. OK?'

'It's a deal,' said Ali.

CHAPTER 15

Ali let himself into the flat. He hung his coat on one of the coat hooks by the door. *That's odd, those hooks weren't there this morning*, he thought.

'Ali?' Mum sounded worried.

Ali walked through into the living room. 'Hi, Mum.'

'Ali! Where have you been?' Mum leapt up off the sofa. She was across the room and squeezing him tight before he had a chance to answer. Then she stepped back. 'I've been worried sick. I told you, you can't just disappear off here. It isn't like Nan's. Dave was attacked, remember?'

'But you knew where I was,' Ali said.

'No, I didn't. You went out this morning to play and I haven't heard from you since. I've been calling all day, but you haven't answered your phone. What was I supposed to think?'

His mobile. He'd left it in Gez's CSI kit. And Gez's mum had taken it.

'It's at Gez's house. I'm sorry.'

'Oh, Ali.' Mum looked cross. 'I got you that so that we could stay in touch. That was the whole point.'

What if Gez saw something during the night? What if he needed to get in touch? 'I'll go and get it,' Ali said. 'It'll only take a second. I'll run straight there and back. And it isn't proper night-time yet.'

Before Mum could argue, Ali left the room and grabbed his coat. He ran out of the front door and into the lift. Then he was back out into the night.

CHAPTER 16

Ali was alone outside the tower block. The yard and the road were deserted. His own ragged breathing was the only sound. The night was like a damp cave, and the stars were hidden by clouds. He leaned back against the door, feeling the solid strength of Lever Tower behind him.

Then he pushed himself off and ran into the gloom.

His footsteps sounded loud, hitting the concrete – *bang, bang, bang, bang.*

Through the yard.

Along the pavement.

To the lane.

The woods looked different in the dark. They were no longer the spindly, thin cover of trees that they were in the daytime. At night, they were the wildwood. Their branches were twisted, clattering bone fingers.

The dry leaves whispered to the night. And the night answered with cries that raised goosebumps on Ali's skin. He slowed to a walk. Then a careful tiptoe. All the while watching the trees. Searching for the shine of eyes staring back at him.

'Hey!' A hand landed heavily on his shoulder.

'Argh!' Ali screamed. The hand tightened. Ali ducked and pulled away. Images flicked through his mind: werewolves, demons, murderers.

'Shh!' the voice said.

'Who's there?' Ali could make out a huge figure, standing in the shadows. An adult. Ali stepped backwards, ready to sprint.

'Ali?' The person stepped forward. 'What are you doing out?'

'Dave?' It was Caitlin's dad. Hanging about the lane in just the place where he'd run into the gang.

'I'm just . . . I have to get my phone,' Ali stammered.

'You shouldn't be here,' Dave said. His voice was cold and hard as ice.

'No. I'm just going.'

'Go home,' Dave said.

Who was Dave to tell him what to do? Dave wasn't his dad. Ali felt a flash of anger burning bright inside. 'I have to get my phone from Gez's.'

Dave shook his head. 'Home. Now.'

89

Ali could make out the thick stubble along his jaw, the darkness around his eyes. His bomber jacket made him look twice the size of a normal person.

'Ali,' Dave's voice held a warning.

'OK, OK. I'm going.' Ali held up his hands.

He stepped away from Dave, then turned and ran back the way he had come. As his feet pounded along the ground, he had the same thought, over and over: *What was Dave doing there?*

CHAPTER 17

Ali was woken early the next morning. Someone was ringing the doorbell. Again and again. He pushed back his duvet and stumbled towards the front door.

'Who is it?' he said.

'Me, Caitlin. Are you ready to go?'

Ali opened the door and rubbed his eyes. Caitlin looked him up and down, her lips pressed together. 'You've got two minutes to get dressed and eat breakfast,' she said. 'Hurry!'

Ali did as he was told. In record time, they were on their bikes, headed for Gez's. He was harder to wake than Ali, but eventually they were all three cycling towards the pet shop.

Caitlin sped out in front, with Falcon running alongside her. Ali did his best to keep up, but he and Gez lagged a little way behind.

'I've never seen her so cross,' Gez panted. 'Not even when I spilt orange juice on her maths book. Or the time I got glue in her hair in Art. Or that time when I lost her shoes.'

'You lost her shoes?'

'Yup. On a school trip. She was furious. Livid. Raging.'

'Like this?'

'No. This is much worse.'

The pet shop was part of a small parade of shops at the edge of the estate. There was a newsagent on one side of the pet shop and a row of terraced houses on the other. By the time that Ali and Gez arrived, Caitlin had got off her bike and leaned it against a lamp post.

Ali and Gez propped their bikes against a board advertising the local paper. *Big Cat Sighting: Hoax or Horror?* read the headline.

'Caitlin! Wait for us!'

Caitlin gripped Falcon's lead. She looked grim and determined.

Ali turned towards the pet shop. The window display was such a higgledy-piggledy mass of wire cages, dusty toys and battered bags of food, it was impossible to see inside. Caitlin walked straight to the door and pushed.

It was locked.

She rattled at the handle, but the door didn't budge. 'But it's the daytime and it's Tuesday. Shops are always open on a Tuesday. I don't get it,' She said.

Ali pushed and then pulled at the handle. It was no good. 'It's not open.'

'Perhaps the door's round the back,' Gez said hopefully.

'Gez . . .' Caitlin spluttered, gesturing, 'the door is right here.'

Gez shrugged. 'I know. But I meant there might be *another* door, one we could spy at. This door is so covered in tatty adverts that we can't see anything.'

Ali nodded. 'Let's try and get round the back. There's probably an alley or something behind these houses.' There was no obvious way through, but deliveries and things had to go somewhere.

They walked past the first house. Suddenly, Falcon darted towards the door. Caitlin tugged her back sharply, but Falcon still struggled, panting and pulling.

'Falcon! Stop it,' Caitlin said.

'She wants to go to that house,' Gez said.

Caitlin looked up at the red-brick terrace. It looked just like the others in the row — net curtains, china trinkets on the windowsill. It was nothing special.

Caitlin gasped.

'What?'

'I know this house,' she whispered. 'It's Miss Osborne's house! That's where Falcon's real owner lives!'

'No!' Ali looked at the house. There was something about it that made the hairs on the back of his neck tingle. It was too still, too quiet, as though it were waiting. Had Miss Osborne been kidnapped from here? Was she being held somewhere, on a boat out at sea, or in the pet shop just next door, against her will?

'Come on.' Gez gave Ali a small prod. 'Let's find the back door.'

A few doors down, there was a left turn that led to an alley. It was bumpy with potholes and weeds. They followed it round to the back of the houses, past a couple of squat garages on the right.

'Which is Miss Osborne's house?' Gez asked.

'The one next to the pet shop,' Caitlin said.

'And which one is the pet shop, smarty-pants?'

'I'm sure we'll recognise it,' Ali said.

Ali was right. It was easy to tell where the row of shops started. There were no fences, and their back yards were all open concrete, like a small car park. There were big bins the size of skips. Piles of stacked cardboard tied up with string leaned against them.

'That's the pet shop. And that one's Miss Osborne's.' Ali pointed.

'What should we do now?'

'Take a peek. See if we can see her, or the gang. But be careful – we don't want anyone to spot us.'

They stepped slowly up to the back of the shop. A thick door was set into the wall, with a barred window next to it. Ali gripped the door handle and turned it slowly. Nothing happened; the door was locked.

'The window,' he whispered. He and Caitlin raised themselves on tiptoe, using the metal bars to steady themselves. Ali pressed his face as near to the glass as he could. The window was dirty, but he could just about make out the room inside. There were piles of boxes against the walls: dog food. There was an open doorway in the far wall. This was just a storeroom. He felt disappointment well up inside. They wouldn't learn anything here. Was there really no clue? He gripped the bars tighter and lifted himself up, wedging his trainers against the brick wall to get a few centimetres higher.

'Look there!' he said.

'What?' Gez, shorter, struggled to see in too.

'There. That door!' Ali jerked his head towards the left side of the room. A wooden door was set into the wall. It was white with an old-fashioned round handle.

Caitlin gripped the bars tightly and leaned into Ali, pushing him to one side. There wasn't enough room for the three of them *and* Falcon all staring in. 'What about it?' she asked.

'Where do you think it leads?'

'Just into the shop, probably,' Gez said.

'No. The doorway straight on goes to the shop. So where can the white door lead?'

'Oh,' Caitlin said slowly. 'I see. It's in the wrong wall, isn't it? It must lead into the house next door!'

'Miss Osborne's house!' Ali let himself drop back to the ground. Caitlin landed beside him.

'Do you think it means something?'

'I don't know. I need to think.'

Just then, Ali heard the sound of an engine and wheels crunching over stones and gravel. 'There's a car coming!' he whispered urgently.

'Hide!' Caitlin tugged his sleeve and pulled him towards the huge bins at the side of the yard. He grabbed Gez on the way past.

'I'm not getting in there!' Gez said.

'Shh. We don't have to get in the bin, just under the cardboard. Come on. Quick!'

Ali dropped down to the ground and shoved a few flat boxes aside. Caitlin and Gez slipped in next to him. He pulled the cardboard back over them all. Falcon growled, but Caitlin's hand on her neck soothed her. The boxes smelled dry, like autumn leaves. Weak sunlight filtered through the cardboard, the colour of tea. It was a tight fit.

'Stop wriggling!' Caitlin said.

Ali froze. His breathing sounded loud; his heartbeat sounded louder! And when Gez spoke it sounded like he was yelling.

'Can you see who it is?'

'Shh! They'll hear us!'

'Yes, but *who* will hear us? Can you see?'

Ali gently leaned to the left, so that he could peek out. A white van had pulled into the yard! He could see the profile of the driver, a man with stubble on his face and head.

'Man and van,' Ali whispered.

'Them?'

'Dunno. I dunno what they look like.' The side of the van was hidden by the cardboard. Gez tried to look too, but the biggest box was balanced right in the way.

Falcon whined.

'Shh!' Ali said. Falcon cocked her head and was quiet.

The van door opened. The man moved out quickly. Across the car park, to the shop door and then inside. He was gone.

Ali's mind was racing now, as well as his heart.

A pet shop, an attempted dognap, an orange top and

a connecting door. And, of course, Dave's strange night-time activities. What did it all mean?

He pushed the cardboard aside slowly and stood up. Caitlin, Gez and Falcon crawled out too.

'Hey,' Caitlin said.

Ali looked over. She had pushed the cardboard back into place and now she was holding a piece of paper. One half of a torn envelope.

'It's a note,' Caitlin said. She passed it to Ali.

'*Monkey Adams. Sunday,*' he read. The words were scrawled in blue pen. It might be useful. 'We should get away from here. The driver might come back. He tucked the note in the back pocket of his jeans and led them back to their bikes.

CHAPTER 18

'Is it a riddle?' Caitlin said. She shifted over on Ali's bed so that she could get a closer look at the torn envelope. 'Or a code?'

'Don't push.' Gez shoved his elbow into her side.

'Stop squabbling,' Ali said, and stood up, taking the note with him.

The door to Ali's room opened. He hid the note quickly behind his back. Mum came in carrying a tray with three glasses balanced on it. 'Juice? I thought you might be thirsty.'

She put the tray down on the desk.

'Thanks, Ali's mum,' Gez said.

Mum laughed. 'I suppose that's an improvement on Mrs Ferguson! My name's Anita.'

Caitlin sipped her drink. 'What flavour's this?'

'Orange and mango. Is that OK?'

Caitlin nodded. 'Yum. I've never had mango before.'

Ali looked at Caitlin. She had gone a bit pink, as though she ws pleased.

'Do you like it?' Mum asked.

'It's lovely. Really lovely.'

'Good.'

The doorbell rang. Mum looked up, then went out of the room to answer it.

Ali took the note from behind his back and stared at it again. It had been scrawled quickly, on the back of a white envelope, as though the person who wrote it was in a hurry. He turned it over in his hands. The envelope was just addressed to the pet shop, typed, with no return address. There was nothing inside. Then Ali noticed something. He sniffed the note.

'What?' Gez asked.

'It's weird,' Ali said, taking in a deep breath. 'It smells kind of bad. But kind of not, too. Smell.' He handed the paper to Gez.

'Yuck! How's that not a bad smell?'

Caitlin sniffed. 'It's a bit like dogs. But that's not what it is.'

'Perhaps it's poison?' Gez said. 'Or drugs? It could be gunpowder, if they're smuggling weapons!'

Ali smiled. 'I suppose it could be any of those things. I've never smelled gunpowder.' He paused. 'Or drugs.

Or poison.'

'Well,' Caitlin said, 'we did find it in a pet shop bin. It isn't going to smell like a bed of roses, is it?'

She had a point. The bin was probably full of poo and mouldy dog food and cat sick. But the note had been next to the bin, not in it.

The door opened.

'Caitlin,' Mum said, 'your dad's here.'

Ali frowned. Dave was here? In the flat? What was he snooping around for?

Caitlin put her glass down on the bedside table and stood up.

'It's OK,' Mum said to Caitlin. 'He doesn't need you home yet. He's after Falcon.' Mum paused. 'In fact, he's asked if I want to take a quick walk with them. I'll just nip out for an hour or so, OK?'

'What?' Ali asked. 'What do you want to do that for?' He looked at Mum. Was she blushing? She was! Ali didn't know what to say. He felt suddenly angry. Dave couldn't just come here and tell Mum what to do. He might be the boss of a bunch of criminals, but he wasn't the boss in this flat!

'I'm just getting a bit of fresh air,' Mum said. 'I won't be long. Come on, Falcon.'

Falcon stood up and followed Mum out of the room.

'Caitlin's dad and Ali's mum up the tree –' Gez sang.

'Shut up!' Ali said.

'K-I-S-S-I-N-G!'

'They are not!' Ali said. It wasn't true. Mum wouldn't go out with Dave. Except she was. But just for a walk. It was normal; people did that sort of thing. She was just being friendly. Ali scowled, but Gez just kept on singing.

'Gez, shut up!'

'What?' Gez asked. 'I'm only saying.'

Ali took a deep breath; he tried to squish down his temper. But it was no good. It rushed out like sparks from a firework. 'Well, don't! My mum isn't going out with anyone. Especially not Dave. OK?'

There was a sudden silence.

He looked at Caitlin. Her face was pale and her eyes sparkled dangerously. 'And what's wrong with my dad?'

Ali bit his lip. 'Nothing. I didn't mean anything.'

'Yes, you did!'

'Look,' Ali said carefully, 'this doesn't matter right now. We need to concentrate on the note. We need to find Miss Osborne before it's too late.'

Gez nodded. 'Yes, come on, Caitlin. Don't start a fight. What do you reckon Monkey Adams is?'

Caitlin nodded slowly, but she still looked cross. 'It

could be a code name,' she said. 'One of the gang, maybe.'

'There was Woody, but I didn't hear any of the others' names,' Gez said. 'It's a shame we've only got half the note.'

'We should go back,' Caitlin said. 'We should look for the other half of the envelope.'

'Yes! We should go back tonight, under cover of darkness!' Gez said.

'Well,' said Ali, 'how about just after tea? It will be dark then, but I'll still be allowed out. Just. How can you get out of the house all the time, without your parents freaking?' Ali asked Gez.

'I have three brothers.' Gez grinned. 'My mum and dad have a problem trying to remember our names, let alone keeping track of where we're all supposed to be. You two should be pleased your parents are getting together. Everyone should have brothers and sisters. It's brilliant.'

Ali threw a pillow at Gez. And this time so did Caitlin.

CHAPTER 19

Ali watched the winter sun set behind the town. The last red and orange streaks made the sky look like fire. Mum still wasn't back from her walk. There was a tight knot in Ali's stomach, as though it was clenched into a fist. Mum had better be all right, that's all. If Dave had hurt her, or kidnapped her, or shown her whatever was inside the boxes and made her an accomplice, then Ali would make him pay.

The front door opened. Mum was back.

'Hi, sweetheart,' she called.

The fist in his stomach screwed tighter. Now it burned. Anger. He didn't reply.

'Ali? Hello?' Mum stood in the doorway. Ali could see her reflected in the windowpane. She was unwinding her pink shawl.

'Hi,' he said finally.

'Anything interesting going on?' Mum asked.

Ali shrugged.

'Well, I've been having a nice time. I walked along the river towards town. There's allotments and the park, you know. All quite close. We should explore together one weekend.'

Ali made a noise that was nearly agreeing.

'Cat got your tongue?' Mum smiled. 'Oh, guess what? We went to a pet shop too. You would've liked that. Perhaps we could go there sometime?'

Ali spun round and looked at Mum properly. 'A pet shop? Why?'

Mum shrugged. 'Dave said it was time for Falcon to go back to her owner. He was delivering her to the people at the pet shop.'

'Falcon's owner was at the pet shop?' Ali stood up. Dave had taken Mum right into the heart of the gang! He had put her in danger.

'No.' Mum shook her head. 'I didn't see her owner. But the men in the shop said they'd look after Falcon until she got back. Ali, what's the matter?'

Ali's fists were clenched so tight that his nails dug into his skin. Red-hot blood pumped around his body. Dave had taken Mum to the shop, had introduced her to his minions.

And, he realised suddenly, Dave had left Falcon

with the men!

Falcon was gone! The gang had got her!

'Ali, what is it? What's the matter?'

Ali took a slow breath. He couldn't tell Mum, she wouldn't understand. 'Nothing. Nothing's wrong. It's just Caitlin. She . . . she really loves Falcon. She's going to be upset.'

'Oh, of course.'

'I'm going to go and see she's OK. All right? I'll be back soon.' Ali grabbed his coat from the hooks.

'Yes, fine,' Mum said. 'But don't go far. It's getting dark.'

Ali leaned hard on Caitlin's doorbell. Inside, he heard its sharp buzz, like a fly hurling itself at a window.

There was no answer.

She wasn't home. Had she found out what her dad had done? Was she angry? Upset? Or did she still not believe that her dad was bad news? Ali gave a short, hard laugh. How could she not believe it? After what Gez heard, and now this! Dave had given Falcon to the bad guys. Ali pressed the bell once more, just to be sure.

Nothing.

Ali lay his hand on the door. The wood was cool and soothing against his palm. He turned away. As he walked back towards the lift, he saw the small flight of stairs that went up to the roof. Caitlin might be hiding up there.

He pushed open the door. It seemed like ages since he'd been here last. But it was only a few days. Then it had been Everest, sunshine on top of the world. Now it was dark and windy, and the sounds of the streets drifted up from below: a police siren, a dog barking, cars driving home.

He stepped out, looking for Caitlin. She was there, standing near the edge, gripping the handrail. She looked out towards the night-lit docks and the sea beyond.

'Caitlin,' Ali said.

She wiped her face quickly with the back of her sleeve.

Was she crying? His anger stalled for a moment. Then he remembered that it was her dad who was causing all this trouble. Her dad who was putting Mum in danger.

'What do you want?' Caitlin asked.

'Mum came back,' Ali said. 'She said Dave had given Falcon away.'

Caitlin's shoulders shook slightly. She was definitely crying.

'I didn't . . . I didn't get to say goodbye,' she said through tears.

Ali opened his mouth, but no words came. It suddenly hit him. Falcon was gone. Dad was gone. Mum might be going. He felt as though there was a black hole sucking away all the things he cared about.

'Dad always lets me say goodbye. He knows how important it is,' Caitlin whispered.

It was all Dave's fault, Ali thought. He was ruining everything. 'Your dad shouldn't have done that,' he said angrily.

Caitlin shrugged. 'Dad thought it was best. For Falcon to go to Miss Osborne's sister.'

Her *sister*? Ali froze. 'Her sister?' he said. 'Was that what he told you?'

Caitlin turned towards him. Tears rolled slowly down her cheeks. She'd given up trying to hide it. She sniffed. 'Yes. He took Falcon to Miss Osborne's sister today. He said it was for the best. I don't know why.'

Dave had lied to Caitlin! He hadn't gone near any sister. He had taken Falcon straight to the men who had tried to kidnap her. The men who were holding her owner! He felt the skin on his arms rise into goosebumps. This was awful.

Ali tried to speak. But the words just wouldn't come. Caitlin already looked so hurt.

'I want to be by myself,' Caitlin said. She turned back to look at the sea.

'Aren't you coming to look for the other half of the envelope?' Ali asked. His anger had vanished; now all he felt was a slow dread.

'No. I don't want to.'

'But we need you,' he said.

'I said, I don't want to.' Caitlin glared at him. 'Oh, go away, Ali. Just leave me alone.'

'But, Caitlin –'

'I said go!'

Ali turned and ran back inside.

CHAPTER 20

Ali took the lift down to the ground floor. He called Gez's mobile.

'Hola?' a strange voice said at the end of the line.

'Oh. I was ringing for Gez.'

'Gez? Wait.' There were a few muffled sounds, and then Ali heard someone yell Gez's name.

A few moments later, Gez spoke breathlessly. 'Hello? Who's that?'

'Gez, it's me, Ali.'

'Oh, hi. Michael's punching me. Some *girl* is going to ring him soon. You have to talk quick.'

'OK. Dave gave Falcon to the pet shop.'

Gez whistled softly.

'He lied to Caitlin,' Ali said. 'I didn't put her straight, but she's mad with me anyway.'

'Why? What did you do?'

'I dunno. Honest. But that isn't even the worst part. Dave took my mum with him when he went to the pet shop. He's getting her involved.'

There was silence at the other end of the line.

'Gez? Are you there?' Ali asked.

'Yes. But I won't be soon. Michael is going to kill me if I don't get off his phone. Listen, we need to go there. To the shop.' Gez paused while he thought. 'OK, listen, here's the new mission. We go to the shop, we find the other half of the envelope. That tells us where to find our targets – Falcon and Miss Osborne. We rescue them and everyone lives happily ever after, except for Dave because he'll be in prison. Easy.'

Ali grinned. 'Anything else?'

'Yes, while we're at the shop we could buy a new pet. Chinchillas are cool.'

'OK. Sounds like a good plan. Meet me outside in two minutes.'

'Roger that, Detective Superintendent.'

Gez sang the theme tune to a cop show as they ran together along the pavement. They dodged people walking yappy dogs, ducked around shopping bags and trolleys, leapt over puddles that reflected the orange street lights. And all the while, car headlights swept across them like search beams.

111

'Drop and roll!' Gez yelled as he weaved past lamp posts. As the next car flashed past, Gez groaned and stumbled. He crackled into an imaginary radio. 'Back-up requested. Officer down.'

Ali smiled. Then took his own radio from his back pocket. 'Roger that, DI Brown. We've got you covered. DS Ferguson, out.'

DS Ferguson helped injured DI Brown up, by the arm, pulling it over his shoulders. He staggered under the weight of his fallen companion. 'Stay with me, DI Brown. We're nearly there.'

Suddenly, Gez's lolling head shot up. He stood up straight and pointed towards the road. 'Look! No way!' he said.

'What?' Ali asked.

'That car! That car! Did you see?'

'Gez! What?' Ali tried to see what Gez was pointing at, but the sleek silver car was pulling away from them.

'That was Jason Adams!'

'What would Liverpool's best striker be doing driving around our estate?' Ali asked.

Gez pulled him forward, after the car. 'I don't know. Perhaps he was visiting his gran. She might live here.'

'He earns thousands of pounds a week. His girl-friend is a pop star. They're in magazines all the time with pictures of their posh house and silly pets. His gran does *not* live here. It can't have been him,' Ali said.

'It was. I'm telling you.'

'No, it wasn't.'

'Yes, it was.'

Ali sighed.

The car was out of sight. And they had reached the parade of shops. Ali put his arm out, barring the way. Gez was silent beside him. 'Target in range,' Ali whispered.

'Any sign of the enemy?' Gez asked.

'Negative,' Ali said. The front of the shop was in darkness. 'Wait!' Ali noticed something. 'Miss Osborne's house – there's a light in the window upstairs!'

'Really?' Gez stood on tiptoe to get a better look. 'Do we have a new target, DS Ferguson?'

Ali thought for a moment. They might find the other half of the envelope in the pet shop. But they might find the whole gang and their hostages in the house next door.

'Affirmative. We'll start with the house. Then go to the cardboard pile. This has to be done quickly and quietly. We try to find out if Miss Osborne's in there and who's holding her. But we don't get caught.'

Gez nodded firmly. 'No, if we get caught my dad'll kill me.'

'Come on.'

The boys crept down the back lane, silent as assassin church mice. Each step was careful and precise. Ali opened Miss Osborne's garden gate slowly. The rusty hinge creaked.

'Shh!' Gez hissed.

'I'm trying!' Ali whispered.

They moved into the garden. In the starlight, they could see an overgrown lawn with brambly borders. There was an apple tree in the centre of the lawn. Beyond that was a small concrete yard with the bin standing guard next to the back door. The house seemed to lean towards them, dark and forbidding.

Ali waved Gez forward. They scurried towards the tree and crouched behind it. Ali felt the damp, crumbly bark beneath his fingertips. He looked at the house. There were no lights on this side of the building. No sign of anyone at all.

'We need to see in upstairs,' Gez whispered. 'I could climb the tree.'

Ali looked up. The first branch was way over their heads. Gez probably couldn't reach it, even if he helped. 'It's too high.'

'Nah. I can stand on the bin. Let's pull it closer.'

Ali nodded. Together they stepped across the yard and grabbed the handles of the wheelie bin. It tilted heavily back on its axis. They pulled it towards the lawn, its wheels rumbling over the concrete. They heaved together and the bin mounted the small rise where the turf began. Then it wobbled.

Ali grabbed the side.

Gez grabbed the lid.

They both pushed upwards. Too hard.

The bin clattered on to its side with a bang that sounded like a car crash in the darkness. The echoes bounced around the garden. Rubbish tumbled on to the ground. Ali grabbed Gez's arm and pulled him back behind the tree. Ali's heart was pounding like a toddler with a saucepan lid. He peered up at the house, desperate to spot any sign of movement.

'Sorry,' Gez whispered.

Ali cringed. This was the noisiest secret mission ever. They might as well kick the door down and tap-dance on the kitchen table.

There was no sound from the house. Maybe they'd gone out. Maybe they'd just left a light on by mistake. And Falcon couldn't be inside – she'd have barked the place down if she'd heard that noise.

They waited for what seemed like for ever, but the house stayed silent.

Ali looked at the bin, lying on its side. It was full. He reached out and grabbed Gez's arm. 'It's full!'

'So?'

'They must have been using this house for ages! If Miss Osborne had really gone on holiday then the bin men would have emptied this by now and there would have been no one home to make more rubbish. They've been holding her for ages. She must be in a terrible state. We have to rescue her.'

'We've got till Sunday. That's four days away. We'll find her.'

'Come on. Let's lift the bin.' Ali sighed. 'Quietly.'

Together they righted the wheelie bin. The black bag that had fallen out was ripped. He could see some of the rubbish poking out. Some paper, a few bits of plastic wrapper. And . . . something strange. He reached out. It was something light and powdery spilling out around the paper. It felt rough between his fingers. Sawdust! That's what it was, fine dust and curls of shaved wood. Had someone been making chairs in Miss Osborne's house while she was away? Or keeping hamsters? He leaned in closer for a better look.

Then the smell hit him.

'Yuck!'

'Shh. What is it?'

'It stinks! Come and smell this.'

'No way!'

'Come on. It smells like the note.'

Gez shuffled over.

'Put your nose there.' Ali pointed to the tear in the bag.

Gez did as he was told. 'Yuck!'

'Told you.'

'What is that?'

'Dunno. It smells like rotten eggs, or blocked loos.'

'Nice.'

'Thanks.' Ali grinned. Then he saw something poking out through the sawdust. White paper. He pulled it out.

'Has it got any writing on it? What does it say?' Gez asked.

'Oh. It's just a receipt. Pizza delivery for Donna. It's probably old. This is like one of those lucky dip things that they have at school fun day.'

'But with poo,' Gez laughed.

Ali caught sight of something else. He pounced. 'It can't be! Look!' He was holding half an envelope, torn and tatty.

'No way!' Gez whispered. 'Does it say anything?'

Ali looked closer. He could make out some writing in blue ink. '*Puma Reynolds. Sunday*,' he read.

'Another code name? Woody, Monkey Adams and Puma Reynolds. Sounds like a cool gang.'

Ali sat back on his heels, looking at the paper in his hands.

'There's something written on the back,' Gez said.

Ali turned the envelope over. Small, spidery writing inched across one corner.

'*Meet do. Saturday. River,*' Gez read. He looked up at Ali. 'Meet do? What does that mean?'

Ali looked harder. There were full stops between the letters. 'It's not do; it's D.O. It's something's initials. Or *someone's* initials.'

Gez gasped. 'Last Saturday Dave O'Connor was walking Falcon by the river. D.O.!' he said.

Suddenly, Ali froze. He could see Gez's face perfectly. Something was wrong. A second ago, they had been in near-darkness. A light had come on in the kitchen. Gez's eyes flashed with panic.

Ali stuffed the envelope into his pocket.

He heard the sound of a kettle boiling.

One of the gang was in the kitchen of Miss Osborne's house, just metres away!

Ali tugged at Gez's sleeve. They had to get out of the garden.

They moved quickly. Too quickly. Gez caught his foot on the shallow kerb. He fell backwards. His legs shot out from underneath him. His trainer caught the side of the bin. The clang vibrated around the garden.

'What the . . . ?' Ali heard a man's voice.

'Gez. Move. Now!' Ali helped Gez to his feet. Together they scrambled towards the gate.

'Hey!' The back door was flung open. A tall rectangle of light hit the garden, framing them clearly. 'Hey! You!' a man shouted.

They were metres away from the gate. Ali heard the man running behind them. He glanced back. The man was just a silhouette in the light from the house. He was gaining on them.

Gez clawed open the gate and dived out. Ali was at his heels. They broke into a sprint, their feet pounding hard. Their breath came in jagged gasps.

And the man was right behind them.

Ali dodged left, then right. He didn't dare look back now. He imagined the man's hand reaching for him, reaching, reaching. Fingers brushing the back of his jacket.

'Faster!' he urged Gez.

The man's footsteps echoed loudly. He was a big man. Heavy. Ali suddenly realised that if they could keep ahead, they could wear him out.

Ali leapt forward. A new strength burned through him. The street passed by in a blur, houses, cars, shops, flashes of shapes and colour. And behind them, relentless footsteps.

Getting quieter.

Ali couldn't bear to turn round. But he was certain of it. The steps were quieter, further away.

'Come on!' he shouted to Gez. It was hard to speak; every breath burned his chest.

They turned a corner, passed an alley. Gez pulled his arm, ducking into the dark space. They leaned against the wall, sucking in air.

Ali waved his arm to quiet them both. He listened. Cars passed, a siren sounded somewhere far away. But there were no footsteps.

'We got away,' Gez whispered. 'That was Woody! Did you see his face when he saw us?'

Ali looked up. He knew where they were. At the end of the alley stood Lever Tower. 'No.' He shook his head. 'I was too busy running. And we haven't got away. We led him straight towards my flat. He knows we were snooping. And he knows we live close by. They'll be looking for us. Dave's gang will be looking for us.'

Later, Ali lay on his bed, the light from his bedside lamp shining on to the envelope in his hands. He turned it over and over.

Puma Reynolds
D.O.

Puma Reynolds

D.O.

Puma Reynolds

Dave O'Connor

He lay back on his bed and stared at the ceiling. What was he going to do?

CHAPTER 21

Gez came round after lunch the next day. He sat on Ali's bed, looking at the torn envelope.

'We have to tell Caitlin about D.O.,' Ali said.

Gez nodded slowly. 'I guess. But does it have to be us that tells her?'

Ali sighed. It wasn't going to be easy, but she *had* to know. He turned away and rested his elbows on the windowsill. It had only been a few days since he'd stood here feeling excited about his new life. And now, that was all gone. Dave had taken it away.

A van rolled slowly down the road just outside Lever Tower.

A white van.

Ali ducked down beneath the sill.

'What? What it is?' Gez asked, standing up.

'Get down! There's a white van out there. It's them,

looking for us.'

'How do you know? There are white vans everywhere. It could just be delivering a fridge to someone for all you know.'

'Gez!' Ali tugged at Gez's jeans, pulling him down.

'OK, OK. Sorry.' There was a pause. 'You don't really think it's them, do you?'

Ali looked at Gez. His face was pale, despite the freckles. 'I don't know. But it could be, couldn't it? That's where Woody lost us yesterday. If I was looking for us, then that's where I'd start.'

'Can you see who's driving?'

Ali rested his fingertips on the windowsill and eased himself up slowly. The van was turning left, back towards the main road. He could only see the rear doors.

'No,' he said. 'Could have been Woody. Could have been Dave.'

'Could have been a guy with a fridge,' Gez added hopefully.

'I don't like it. I think we should stay inside for a while, undercover. Hope they forget about us. And don't wear any of the clothes you were wearing last night.'

Gez looked down. 'But I *am* wearing the clothes I wore last night!'

'Well, go home and change. And find a hat or something, a disguise. But mostly, stay indoors.'

'I can't stay indoors for the rest of my life. I'd go insane, like a caged animal. I need my freedom,' Gez said.

Ali smiled grimly. 'It's not for ever, don't worry. It's just until we can stop Dave.'

'Are you going to speak to Caitlin? Tell her what we found?'

Ali thought about it. He knew he had to tell her, but did he need to tell her right now?

'Maybe,' he said. 'I should probably keep out of Dave's way too, though. Keep a low profile.'

'You mean hide?' Gez asked.

'Yes,' Ali said. That sounded safest.

CHAPTER 22

Once Gez had left, Ali scrunched up his clothes from the night before and stuffed them in the bottom of his wardrobe. He sat on the floor next to his bed. Well away from the window.

'Ali!' Mum shouted from the kitchen.

'Yes?' he yelled back.

'I'm making pancakes. Do you want to help?'

Pancakes? Ali got up and wandered into the kitchen.

'Pancakes? Really?' Ali asked. 'Isn't pancakes just for breakfast on your birthday?'

'No.' Mum laughed. 'We can have pancakes if we want. Whenever we want.'

Ali sat down at the table and smiled. This is exactly how he'd thought it would be, living with Mum by himself. The anxious feeling he'd had since he'd spotted the van started to fade a little.

Soon, Mum was whisking a mixture in the big jug. She poured out a measure on to the frying pan and swirled it around. It smelled great.

'There's some syrup in the cupboard there,' Mum said. 'Or you could slice a banana.'

Ali got up to help. 'Can I toss it?' he asked.

Mum laughed again. 'I don't know,' she said, and passed him the handle of the pan. '*Can* you toss it?'

Ali took the pan and gave it a gentle shake. The pancake was a perfect circle and it slipped around easily. He took a deep breath, steadying himself. He gave it another shake.

'Go on,' Mum said. 'Go for it.'

Ali grinned. Then he flipped the pan up sharply. The pancake whirled up in the air, turning over as it did. Then, *plop*, he caught it back in the pan.

'Woo-hoo!' Mum said.

A moment later, Ali sat back at the table, slicing half a banana on to his pancake. Mum made a second one for herself, then sat down next to him.

'Actually, Ali, it is kind of a special day today,' she said.

Ali looked at her. Her eyes were twinkling and she was smiling.

'I got a call this morning. From Dave.'

Dave? The anxious feeling was back. 'What did he want?'

'Well, us actually. He wants us to go out with him and Caitlin tomorrow. On a day trip. That would be cool, wouldn't it?'

A day trip? A whole day watching Dave smarm up to Mum, telling lies to everyone? No, it didn't sound like fun. And if Woody had told Dave about two boys nosing around, then perhaps Dave suspected Ali. Perhaps Dave was spying on him. Ali felt as though a trap was closing tightly around him. He pushed his plate away, the pancake only half-eaten.

'Aren't you going to finish that?' Mum asked.

'I'm not hungry,' Ali said.

Mum looked at him, frowning, but she didn't say anything.

CHAPTER 23

Ali left his half-pancake and went back into his bedroom. He could hear Mum singing as she did the washing-up. He lay down on his bed and took down his old, battered *Giant Atlas of World Animals* and opened it on the first page. The inscription read:

To Ali, happy 6th birthday. All my love, Dad xxx

Looking at the signature made Ali's eyes prickle with tears. Dad.

What was Dad doing right now? Ali couldn't even guess. It had been nearly six months since the last post-card. He turned to Chapter 5: Asia. There was Dad's card, slipped between the pages, just where he'd left it.

He flipped it over and read the message, even though he already knew it by heart.

Dear Ali,

I am in Bali. I stayed three nights at this temple. There are hundreds of monkeys here. They climb all over the walls and they'll steal your sandwiches if you're not careful!

   Take care,

   Dad

That was all.

Ali must have read it a hundred times, and every time he looked for a clue that told him Dad missed Ali as much as Ali missed Dad. He hadn't found one yet.

He put the postcard back inside the book.

Dad wasn't coming back. He knew that. Dad was making a new life on the other side of the world. Perhaps Mum was right and they should be making a new life too. But why did that have to mean Dave? Why couldn't it just be him and Mum making a new life together?

He put the book back on the shelf.

Perhaps he could go and stay with Dad. It would be nice to visit Asia. He must have distant cousins there.

He almost laughed. He didn't even know which country Dad was in. There was no way he could go and live with him.

No. It was him and Mum. And Dave. And Dave was

trouble. It was up to Ali to stay here and keep Mum safe. Whatever that might take.

They were all going on a day trip. And Ali would be looking out for Mum every minute. Dave was not going to hurt Mum. Not while Ali was around.

CHAPTER 24

Ali woke up slowly. His eyes felt heavy and his body was tired. He lay in bed not moving. Something bad was coming. The thought shot through him like an electric shock, forcing him awake. He remembered. Today, Dave was taking them out. A whole day with the enemy. Ali sighed.

Above him on the bookshelf, he could see the ragged spine of the *Giant Atlas of World Animals*. He had hidden the two halves of the envelope in there, next to his postcard from Dad.

Monkey Adams. Sunday.

Puma Reynolds. Sunday

Meet D.O. Saturday. River.

An image of the scrawled handwriting was burned into his mind. He didn't even have to look at it to remember the words.

They had only two more days before something dreadful happened to Miss Osborne. He would watch Dave like a hawk with binoculars for any clue to where she was being held.

The doorbell rang.

'Oh! That's them,' Mum shouted from her bedroom. 'Ali, are you up? Go and let them in. I'm just finishing getting ready.'

Ali pulled on his jeans and a jumper and went to answer the door. He opened it slowly.

Dave stood there, smiling. The bruise on his face had matured to a mouldy cheese colour. His gold tooth twinkled.

Caitlin held his hand. She smiled a little at Ali. Ali couldn't look her in the eye. He and Gez hadn't told her about the D.O. note yet.

'Hey there, sonny. Mum ready?' Dave said.

'She's just getting shoes.'

'Good.' There was a pause. 'So can we come in then?'

'Oh.' Ali stepped aside and let Dave and Caitlin walk ahead of him. Dave turned right, into the kitchen.

'Everything all right? Got everything you need for your new home?' Dave asked a bit too loudly.

'Fine.' Ali shrugged.

'I like this flat,' Caitlin said, looking up at Dave. 'It

smells like flowers and spices.'

Dave grinned back at her.

Flowers and spices? It was just the air freshener Mum plugged in all over the place! Caitlin made it sound like the Hanging Gardens of Babylon. Ali grabbed and peeled a banana. He scowled. No one noticed.

'Hi, everyone.' Mum stepped into the kitchen. Caitlin smiled shyly, but Dave beamed.

'You look lovely,' he said.

Ali looked at Mum. Actually, Dave was right. She did look lovely. She had washed and straightened her hair, so that it hung like a thick black waterfall. And she had done her make-up. She never wore make-up in the daytime! Ali's stomach tightened. He didn't want the banana now. He put it on the side.

'Not going to finish that?' Dave asked.

Ali shook his head.

'Well, in that case, mind if I do? Haven't had time for breakfast yet.' Dave took the fruit and bit a huge chunk off. Three chews later, the banana was gone. 'Right then. Day of fun-packed adventure, here we come,' he announced.

'The zoo is not my idea of a fun-packed adventure,' Ali whispered to Mum as they stepped out of the car.

'Since when?' she said. 'You'll love it, you know you will. Dave suggested this because I told him how much you like animals. Give this a chance, Ali, please. For me.'

Mum's eyes were pleading. Ali nodded quickly, but didn't speak.

The car park was full. There were families everywhere. The queue at the ticket desk stretched like a snake out across the foyer.

'No problemo,' Dave said when he saw how many people were in front of them. 'I know someone who can get us in for free. Dave O'Connor queues for no man! Wait here.' He moved off.

'Who does he know?' Ali asked Caitlin.

'Everyone.' Caitlin grinned. 'He never pays for anything if he can help it.'

It only took a minute. Then Dave was back, waving four tickets and a map. He was grinning at them all.

'Oh, well done,' Mum said.

'Anything for you, princess,' Dave said.

Yuck. Even Caitlin rolled her eyes.

'Come on,' Mum said, blushing slightly. 'Last to spot a leopard is the loser.'

Ali walked slowly towards the entrance. The others all moved past him. And, he noticed, Caitlin was holding Mum's hand! And they were both laughing at some joke of Dave's. They looked all happy, like something off a washing powder advert.

Dave turned. 'Come on, Al. Don't be a slowcoach.'

Ali scowled, but sped up.

Everyone else looked at the animals. Ali looked at Dave. Did he look like a criminal mastermind? There was his gold tooth, but maybe that was just down to poor dental hygiene. And there were his tattoos, of course. In films, criminal gangs always had the same tattoo, so that they could recognise each other. Were any of Dave's tattoos like that? The bluebird stretched up from under his jacket to just below his hair. His knuckles had letters on them: L-O-V-E on each hand. Was that significant?

'Thinking of getting a tat, sonny?' Dave laughed. 'You're still a bit young for it. But when you're sixteen I could recommend a good artist.'

Ali looked away quickly.

Dave held up the map so that everyone could see it. 'Big cats, or monkeys?' he asked.

'Duh,' Mum said. 'Both.'

It was at the big-cat enclosure that the hair on the back of Ali's neck bristled. Cold shivers shot up his spine. He looked around quickly. Dave was pointing something out to Mum. They were laughing.

135

But that wasn't what was making him nervous.

What was it? He knew, he just *knew*, that something was wrong.

He looked towards the enclosure. The strange yellow eyes of a lion locked on his. It yawned, lolling its red tongue around its razor teeth. Was that it? The slavering jaws of a predator just metres away? That would probably do it, he thought.

He stood perfectly still. There was something not right. He could feel it, like a strange extra sense making his breath catch in his throat. It was like the taste, or the smell of danger.

And then he knew what it was. The smell.

His nostrils were filled with a musty, sweet smell.

A musty, sweet smell that he recognised.

The lion's enclosure smelled exactly like the notes they'd found!

Puma Reynolds.

His brain suddenly felt like it was fizzing with electricity as the connection became clear.

Puma Reynolds!

Those notes weren't a list of gangsters. They weren't nicknames. They were shopping lists! The puma was a real, live puma, leaving its scent around just like these lions were! Dave's gang must be smuggling in wild animals and then making money selling them on. Ali felt that he *had* to be right! Dave must have delivered a puma to someone called Reynolds, and Woody or someone had written the delivery day on the back of an envelope. The same with Monkey Adams! And they'd thrown the note away in two different bins to hide the evidence. But it still had that smell! The smell of a big cat.

Ali imagined a puma crouching inside a box or crate. Its sleek brown fur shining in the darkness. Frightened. Not knowing what was happening to it. Perhaps it had yelped or whined as it was carried off the boat.

Ali remembered what Gez had said about the foxes. They had all disappeared. Perhaps the scent had frightened them away? And it wasn't just the foxes who were scared! There was the headline too, the one he'd seen outside the newsagents: *Big Cat Sighting: Hoax or Horror?* Someone had seen a big cat and reported it to the papers. And he had propped his bike against the biggest clue they'd had! Someone had actually seen the puma. It must have been out, wandering around their estate. Mr Reynolds' puma.

All of a sudden, his legs felt wobbly. Ali looked around for a chair. There was a plastic one shaped like a giraffe nearby. He dropped down into it.

Over by the enclosure, Dave slung his arm around

Caitlin's shoulder. Did Dave capture the animals himself? Or did he pay other people to do it? To trap the wild things and steal them away? Ali felt his anger rise, hot and livid. He glared at Dave's back. It wasn't right. It wasn't right at all. Ali gripped the edge of the seat, trying to stay calm. If Dave was suspicious of Ali, then it was a bad idea to be behaving weird.

'Ali? Are you OK?' Mum asked.

'Er . . .'

'You look really pale.'

Ali felt Mum's hand on his forehead.

'You're clammy. Do you feel poorly?'

Ali managed to focus his attention on to Mum. Her eyes were full of concern. 'I'm OK,' he managed to say. 'Really. Just a bit tired. All the walking.'

'Yes. I think it's time for a snack. You had no breakfast. Come on, everyone, let's find some sugar!'

Ali struggled to his feet.

Caitlin fell into step beside him. 'What's the matter? Allergic to cats?' she asked.

Ali slowed, letting Dave and Mum walk ahead. 'I know what the pet shop gang are doing,' he whispered fiercely.

'No!'

'Shh, not so loud. It was the smell. Of the lions. Did you get a whiff? It smells just like the note.'

138

'They're making paper from lion poo?' Caitlin said, laughing.

'What? No. They're smuggling animals. Catching them in the wild and bringing them by boat to here. Then selling them.'

'What do you mean? How do you know?' she asked.

'The note. It all fits, I'm telling you. The note, the foxes, the headline. Everything.'

'What are you talking about? Who'd want to buy wild animals?'

Ali shrugged. 'Could be anyone. Rich people. Footballers, actors, singers.' He glared at Dave's back. Then he gasped. 'Jason Adams! Gez thought he saw him on the estate, but I told him he was imagining things. He must have been there to buy something from the gang.'

'Jason Adams?' Caitlin asked, struggling to keep up.

'A monkey!' Ali shrieked. 'He must have been buying a monkey. Monkey Adams!'

Caitlin nodded slowly. 'His girlfriend is always in magazines carrying a dog in a handbag. Perhaps she wanted something even cuter. Do you really think that's what the gang are doing?'

'I'm sure of it.' Ali said.

'Do you think they took Miss Osborne because she tried to stop them?'

'I don't know.'

Should he tell Caitlin that they had Falcon? And what about the D.O. note? Somehow he'd ended up keeping secrets from Caitlin that he hadn't meant to keep at all. He had to tell her that Dave was in charge. He had to make her believe it.

'We have to stop them,' Caitlin said.

Ali nodded slowly.

'Come on, you two,' Mum shouted. 'There's a hot-chocolate stand here. What would you like?'

This wasn't the right time to tell Caitlin, Ali thought. It wasn't fair. But he had to tell her and he had to tell her soon.

Perhaps he should ask Gez what he thought first.

CHAPTER 25

Dave drove them back to the flats just as the sun was setting. Ali and Caitlin hardly spoke on the ride home. Ali felt that there was too much inside his head for him to be able to talk about the zoo animals or how nice lunch had been, or any of the other things that Mum kept going on about.

As soon as they'd unclicked their seat belts, Ali and Caitlin jumped out. Caitlin skipped away from the car. 'I'm just going to play out for a little while, Dad,' she said.

Dave nodded and walked towards the flats.

'Me too,' Ali said. 'If that's OK.'

Mum paused. Her forehead creased. She held Ali's shoulder and looked at him closely. 'Is everything all right?' she asked. 'You were really quiet today.'

'I'm fine, Mum. Honest.'

'Listen. I know it must be weird for you. A day out with someone who isn't your dad. But you should give Dave a chance, you know. Perhaps we should chat about it?'

Ali's eyes widened. He'd discovered that Dave was the criminal mastermind of an international animal-smuggling ring, and Mum wanted to talk about *feelings*. There was nothing to talk about! 'Mum. I'm fine. I just need to see Gez for a bit. I won't be long.'

'Ali, do you like Dave?'

Ali looked towards the flats. Dave was holding open the main door. He was too far away to hear.

How could he tell Mum that it wasn't a question of *liking* Dave? Perhaps Dave was a lovely person, *if* you ignored the fact that he took animals from the wild. Perhaps he was lots of fun, *if* you ignored the fact that he had Miss Osborne locked up somewhere. Perhaps he was really kind, *if* you ignored the fact that he told lies to his own daughter.

'Mum, please . . .'

Mum shook her head. 'Oh, go on then. But don't be late. Fish fingers for tea in an hour.'

They found Gez in his den. He had arranged action figures along the top of one of the crates; they were firing down at a battalion of woodlice below.

'Gez,' Caitlin said, as she pushed her way through the brambles, 'we've worked it out.'

'Well, good for you,' Gez said. 'I hope you've had a lovely day investigating.'

'What?' Ali asked.

'I hope you've had a brilliant time together, working it out. I'm glad I wasn't there to get in the way of all that hard thinking.'

'Gez?' Caitlin said, sounding hurt.

Ali grinned. 'You're cross with us because you missed us!'

'I did not.'

'Yes, you did!' Ali said.

'I've been too busy even to notice you two weren't here. Look –' he pointed at the crate – 'my soldiers are defending the last tower as the alien army advances. We were just about to defeat them when you two showed up and distracted the general. I'm the general, by the way.'

'Oh, don't be cross,' Caitlin said. 'We only went to the boring zoo. Dad wanted us to *bond*. And it helped us to work things out, but apart from that it was really rubbish.'

'Honest?' Gez asked hopefully.

'Yes,' Ali said. 'Totally rubbish. Now listen.'

Ali took a few minutes to explain to Gez all that he

had worked out. He was careful not to mention Dave's name in front of Caitlin. He didn't want Caitlin and Gez to be upset with him at the same time. Gez sat down heavily on the crate, knocking what was left of the defending soldiers on to the ground.

'So,' Gez said, 'pumas and monkeys and . . . and who knows what else were being smuggled past my den in the middle of the night by an evil gang. And *I slept right through it!*' His voice rose in disbelief.

'Yup,' Ali said. 'But right now we need to know two things –'

'How to stop them,' Gez interrupted.

'And how to rescue Miss Osborne. She only has until the day after tomorrow,' Caitlin added.

'Exactly. It's been nearly a week since Gez first saw them,' Ali said. 'Perhaps they come every weekend.'

Gez grinned. 'It's the weekend tomorrow. We should be there as a welcoming committee. Tomorrow night we take them down.' He reached for one of the action figures and aimed its gun towards the river. 'Pow, pow, pow. No one smuggles wild beasts past my house and gets away with it.'

CHAPTER 26

The next morning, Ali walked to Gez's house.

He found Gez in the back garden. He was kicking at the garden's spiky hedge.

'What did it do?' Ali asked, pointing to the hedge. 'Insult your mum?'

Gez grinned, then eased a battered football out of a hedge with the end of his trainer. 'Nope. It ate my football, but I've got it back now.' He knocked it to Ali, who passed it back. 'You here to plan tonight?' Gez asked. 'What do you think the gang'll bring in? A jaguar? An elephant?'

'Dunno,' Ali said.

'You don't sound very excited!'

'We have to tell Caitlin about Dave, we have to show her the D.O. note and we have to tell her that Falcon isn't with Miss Osborne's sister.'

145

'I can't. I'm too young to die,' Gez said, heading the ball to Ali.

'We have to. Even if she gets angry. She can't find out at the pet shop tonight. We have to do it now.' Ali tapped the ball back towards the hedge. 'Come on.'

It took them a while to find Caitlin. No one answered the doorbell at her flat. They couldn't see her around the tower block.

'Roof,' Ali said.

A few moments later, they were walking out on to the roof. Caitlin was there, sitting with her back against the wall, her head resting on her knees. Ali sighed, then walked towards her.

'Wow! Wow! Wow!'

Ali turned.

Gez hadn't followed him. He was standing on the spot, his mouth hanging open. 'Wow! Wow! And wow again! How come no one ever told me this was here? Hey, guys! How come you let me carry on using the hedge down there as a den when you knew this was here? This is amazing.'

'Hi,' Ali said to Caitlin, ignoring Gez.

Nothing.

'Are you OK?' Ali asked. Last time he had been up here, Caitlin had just found out that Falcon had gone.

And he had found out that Dave was a liar.

Gez ran over to the railings. 'You can see the sea from here. It's brilliant. I can see a ship!' he yelled. 'A big green tanker, just out to sea. It could be them. Just think. That ship could have sailed from Borneo or Madagascar or Timbuktu with a cargo of beasts. And tonight the animals will be on a rowing boat coming up our river. Like a tiny little illegal Noah's Ark.'

Ali sat down next to Caitlin. 'Has something happened?' Perhaps she had already found out about Dave. Ali almost felt relieved.

Caitlin shook her head. 'No, nothing's happened. I just came to get some peace. To think.'

'About what?' Ali asked.

'Dad.'

She did know! Ali sighed. 'It must have been tough. Finding out what he's been up to. I'm sorry.'

'No, I'm pleased. I think.'

'What? How can you be pleased?' Ali couldn't believe it!

'But I am. I think it's nice that he's met someone he likes. You should be pleased too, for your mum.'

'Caitlin, what are you talking about?'

Caitlin looked at him properly. 'Dad and your mum, of course. He had such a nice time yesterday that he's asked her out tonight. And she's said yes. It's a date. A proper, official date. I just wanted to come up here and think about it for a while, that's all. I'm pleased really.'

Ali felt as though the concrete floor had slid away from underneath him. 'Mum's going on a date tonight? With Dave?' He shook his head. 'She can't!'

Gez ran closer. 'Did I hear right? Dave's taking your mum with him tonight? Wow. She must be brave. What if it is a jaguar?'

Caitlin stood up, her hands wedged firmly on her hips. 'What are you talking about?'

Gez bit his lip. 'Oops.'

Ali took a deep breath. 'Caitlin, there's something we should have told you before. Two things, in fact. It's just been hard to find a good time to say it.'

Caitlin scowled. 'Come on then, spit it out.'

Ali looked towards Gez, who nodded solemnly. 'OK, here goes. Dave took Falcon to the pet shop, not to Miss Osborne's sister. And we found the other half of the envelope. It said the gang were meeting someone with the initials D.O. at the river. Caitlin, I'm really sorry, but your dad *is* involved in this. Perhaps in charge.'

Caitlin laughed.

That was not the reaction Ali had been expecting. 'It's true,' he said

'No,' Catlin said firmly. 'No, it isn't. No way.'

'But it is!' Gez said. 'I heard them talking about him.'

Caitlin stopped laughing as quickly as she'd started. 'It isn't true.' Her voice was as cold as the air around them. 'Dad would never do that. Never. He loves animals.'

'Caitlin,' Ali said, 'I saw him by the river, just standing and waiting at night. He was waiting for the gang.'

'Ali! My dad got hurt by those men. Have you forgotten that? They attacked him!'

'Mutiny,' Gez said, in little more than a whisper.

'You shut up, Gez Brown! My dad is not a criminal. Well, not a big one, anyway. He wouldn't do something like this.' She glared at Ali. 'You're only saying it because you don't want him to go out with your mum.'

'No, I'm not,' Ali said.

'Yes, you are. You don't think he's good enough for your mum. But at least he's *here*, which is more than you can say for your precious dad.' Caitlin's eyes widened and she held a hand to her mouth. 'Oh.'

But she had said it.

Ali's eyes were suddenly hot and wet. He pressed his fingertips against his eyelids. He could see the piercing blue of his dad's eyes in the darkness. He tried to conjure the rest of his dad's face. But he couldn't do it.

He couldn't remember what Dad looked like. He turned away from the others, walked towards the wall and pressed his hands against the cold, solid concrete.

'Ali, I'm sorry,' Caitlin said. 'I didn't mean that. I only said it because I was angry. But you're wrong about Dad. I know you are. And I'll prove it to you tonight.'

There was a silence. The cries of a seagull above them sounded like someone in pain.

Gez gave an embarrassed cough. 'Well,' he said, 'we'll need a plan. *Whoever's* holding Miss Osborne and bringing in the animals will be at the river. And we'll be there to watch them.'

'No,' Caitlin said. 'We'll be there to stop them.'

Ali breathed slowly. He turned back to the others. Caitlin looked at him shamed-faced. He tried to give her a smile, but it felt weak.

She smiled back. 'Ali,' she said gently, 'Dad's sorting out a babysitter for us tonight.'

'Oh,' Ali said, wondering what she was getting at.

'I'll tell him not to. Gez, you should have a sleep-over. Invite me and Ali.'

'OK, when?'

'Tonight, of course. Then we'll be able to sneak out together. Will your mum mind us staying?'

'No. There's always loads of people in my house. She

probably won't even notice.'

'Good,' Ali said. 'What time should we meet? And what should I bring?'

'Come to mine at six, for tea,' Gez said. 'Wear dark clothes. We should dress like ninjas.'

'And we'll need bikes. Let's store them in the den. I'll bring my mobile. We might have to call the police.'

'Excellent,' Gez said. 'This gang is going down!'

CHAPTER 27

'How do I look?' Mum twirled around the living room. She was wearing a blue silk tunic over embroidered jeans.

Mum was in danger. The thought was like a pulse, throbbing inside Ali. She was in danger and he had to save her.

Outside, the sun was setting and the sky was the livid purple of a bruise.

'Nice,' Ali said finally.

'Oh, Ali.' Mum sat down next to him on the sofa. 'This is hard for you, isn't it?' She brushed his cheek with her fingertips. 'You know I love you, don't you?'

Ali nodded. 'Mum . . . I don't think you should go out with Dave tonight. I don't think you should go out with him at all.' The words came out in a rush.

'Ali, is it because of Dad? Because he's gone, you

know. He's gone.'

'I know that!' Ali hadn't meant to shout. 'I know,' he said more quietly. 'It isn't because of Dad. It's Dave. He's no good – I just know it. I can't prove it yet, but I will.'

'No.' Mum's voice was firm. 'You have to stop this. You haven't even given him a chance.'

'But –'

'I mean it. I want you to stop being so hard on him. Give him a chance. For me.'

Ali pressed his lips closed. It was no good. Mum wouldn't believe him, unless he showed her. So, he'd just have to show her.

He took a deep breath. 'You look really nice,' he said.

'Thank you,' Mum dropped a kiss on his forehead. 'Are you ready to go to Gez's house?'

Ali nodded. He had found black clothes, he had charged his mobile, he was ready. *I am a ninja*, he thought. He'd have to be; Mum was relying on him, whether she knew it or not.

CHAPTER 28

Ali knocked on Gez's back door.

'Operation Follow the Baddies is go,' Gez said happily when he let Ali in.

Ali stepped into the kitchen. 'Shh!' he said. 'Everyone will hear you.'

'It wouldn't matter if they did. They'd only think it was some silly game I'm playing. They never take me seriously. It's brilliant. Watch this.' He walked into the living room, where Ali could see Gez's mum sitting on the sofa.

'Mum . . .' Gez said. 'Mum, I thought me and Ali could go and hunt some criminals later. Some smugglers or kidnappers. Is that OK?'

Gez's mum chuckled, 'Of course it is, sweetheart. Just don't make too much mess, OK?'

Gez grinned at Ali. 'See?'

Ali laughed. Now they had permission! He followed Gez up the stairs into his bedroom.

'Is Caitlin here?' Ali asked, looking around.

'No, not yet. She'll be here any minute though.'

'Do you think she'll still be cross with us?'

'Yes.'

'Oh.' Ali sat on Gez's bed. 'Cool snake,' he said, nodding a quick hello to Percy.

'Hello?' Caitlin's voice came yelling up the stairs. She must have let herself in.

Gez went to the bedroom door. 'We're in here.'

Caitlin came up. She carried a huge black sports bag; she needed two hands to keep it on her shoulder.

'What have you got there?' Ali asked.

'Supplies,' she said, dropping the bag to the floor. 'Everything we need to prove Dad's innocence.'

Ali and Gez flashed a look to each other. She was still cross.

'I've got biscuits, apples, a torch, a blanket,' Caitlin said. 'Some dog food in case the animals are hungry, a tin opener, a bowl, a bottle of water, and some rope.'

'Rope?' Ali asked.

'Well, you never know, we might have to tie some bad guys to a chair or something,' Caitlin said.

'Or abseil down a tall building!' Gez said.

'OK, rope. Fair enough,' Ali said. 'We can take turns

carrying the bag. It looks heavy.'

'Good idea,' Caitlin said. '*Teamwork.*' Her voice dripped sarcasm.

'Oh, don't be like that, Caitlin,' Gez said. 'It's not our fault your dad's a criminal.'

'Argh! You are just a nightmare, Gez Brown. You wait. You just wait!'

The evening passed quickly. They ate tea with Gez's family, all eight of them squished into the living room with plates on their laps. Then they played a racing game on the computer, until one of Gez's brothers stole the controls. Caitlin tried to teach them rummy, but it was too hard to concentrate with the noise of Gez's big brothers arguing. Suddenly, it was quarter to ten.

'How are we going to get out of the house?' Ali whispered.

'Easy. We say, "Goodnight." Then we put pillows and stuff into the beds and turn off the light. No one will notice.'

'What about Michael and Owen? They'll notice when they come to bed?'

'Nah. And anyway, if they do, they won't tell Mum. It's too good a thing to blackmail me with. I'll be doing their chores for months. They won't tell – at least, not tonight. Don't worry, it will be easy.'

Ali was amazed to find that Gez was right. They made a big show of going up to bed, but no one seemed to pay any attention. Gez's mum and dad waved them upstairs, but didn't come to tuck them in like his own mum would have.

'OK,' Gez whispered from his bed. 'This is the tricky part. We'll have to climb out the window.'

'The window?' Caitlin yelped. 'But we're on the first floor!'

'Yeah, I know. But the kitchen roof is below us. We can lower ourselves down on to that and it's easy to get down into the garden from there. I do it all the time. Get your beds ready.'

Ali tucked a spare pillow under his duvet. In the gloom it almost looked like a sleeping person. He tried to sculpt it a little bit, but it was no good. If anyone turned the light on, it would be obvious that there was a pile of goose feathers in the bed instead of him. He just hoped no one would. And that he, Caitlin and Gez would be back safely before morning.

It was trickier to get down to the garden. Gez went first, to show them how it was done. Then it was Ali's turn. As he climbed out, flecks of paint from the windowsill came off in his hands. Despite the cold, his palms were sweaty. He probed for the roof with his toes, flailing in midair. Then, underfoot, he felt the solid shape of the slates. He let go of the sill slowly, trusting that the roof would hold and that he wouldn't go falling through on to Gez's mum's kitchen table below.

He inched along the tiles, his trainers squeaking on the cold surface. And then, suddenly, the slate seemed to move underneath him. He felt himself slipping down. He grabbed wildly, but just clutched the air. He scrabbled to stay upright. He spun, rolled and fell. He slid off the roof and landed heavily on the grass. The air was knocked out of him. He lay still.

'Ali?' He heard Caitlin moving quickly on the roof. Then she was next to him, her hand on his forehead. 'Ali? Are you dead?'

Ali groaned. Then he rolled on to his back. He could see the outline of Caitlin's face framed by stars. Gez was beside her.

'You idiot!' Gez whispered. 'That was not ninja-like at all. Caitlin did it much better. Have you broken anything?'

Ali sat up slowly. He ached a bit, but nothing felt too bad. 'No. I'm OK,' he said.

'Good. Come on, let's catch some baddies. If we get to the den quickly, we can have a midnight feast before they arrive. There should be enough time.'

'Trust you to be thinking of your stomach,' Caitlin said.

'Shh. Let's go.' Gez led the way out of the garden into the back lane. The road was deserted. Once his eyes adjusted to the moonlight, he could see the path to the river. The water was loud in the darkness, as though the river was high and swollen.

They moved as quietly as they could, off the path and into the den. The log and the crate were damp with dew, but Gez sat down anyway.

'Can I have one of the biscuits?' he asked.

Caitlin opened her bag. Then paused. 'Did you hear that?' she asked.

'What?' Then Ali heard it. The drone of an engine. Coming from the lane.

'It's them!' Caitlin said. She closed her bag and stood, ready to move out.

'Wait,' Ali said. 'We know these people are danger-ous. We can't just barge up to them and ask them to let the animals go. We have to wait and watch. We follow them until we know where Miss Osborne is. Then we call the police. The police come and arrest them and we go home without anyone noticing we've been gone. OK?'

'OK,' Gez said. He saw Caitlin nod silently.

This was like a game of cat and mouse, Ali thought. He just hoped that tonight the cats weren't too big.

CHAPTER 29

They edged their way quietly out of the den, towards
the water. Whoever was meeting Dave would be
landing there. The thick brambles clawed at Ali's legs,
pulling him back. He forced his way through, trying
not to make a sound. He could hear the other two
breathing behind him.

From the road, he heard the clank of a van door
opening. Down by the water, an owl hooted. Was it a
signal? Ali wondered.

They had reached the edge of the wood. The river
path was just a few steps in front of them; it was bright
and clear in the moonlight. Ali crouched down in the
bushes. His heart was beating so loudly he felt certain
that the men would be able to hear it. Caitlin and Gez
crouched beside him. He felt better knowing they were
there with him.

There was a sudden noise. Scuffling. Coming from the water's edge. Someone was struggling to lift something heavy.

Ali peered out on to the path. It was empty, no one in sight. Then a small torch beam shone out. Someone was coming; the van driver was headed their way! Ali gripped Caitlin's arm. What if it was Dave? Would Caitlin run out? He felt her shrug him off.

Then two shapes moved into the torchlight. Two men coming from the river. They were carrying something between them. Ali caught quick flashes of whatever it was in the torch beam. It was brown. Wicker. It was a basket. And there was something inside it – he heard a creak as the *something* moved.

Then the torch moved upwards. Ali gasped. The man carrying the basket was the same man who had chased him and Gez away from Miss Osborne's house. Woody.

'Hey!' Woody said. 'Get that torch out of my eyes, Sidney. You're blinding me.'

'Sorry. Everything all right?' said the man holding the torch in a deep, gravelly voice.

'Got a real live one here for you,' Woody chuckled. 'Proper dangerous. And hell-bent on escaping. Ain't he, Peep?'

The man carrying the other handle of the basket

started laughing. Woody and Peep lowered the basket to the ground. Ali saw the lid rise, slowly, slowly. Then one furry arm stretched out. It had long, curved claws and moved as though it was half asleep.

'You've not even got a lock on it! It's getting away!' Sidney said.

'Nah,' Woody said. 'Watch.'

A second arm raised itself and eased itself over the edge of the basket. The wicker wobbled, and then toppled on to its side. A head about the size of a melon peered out. Sensing freedom, the animal moved as fast as its legs could carry it.

Sidney started laughing too. 'Oh, I see.'

The animal had moved about ten centimetres away from the basket, lifting each heavy limb in turn.

'Yes,' Woody said. 'The amazing three-toed sloth. Top speed of one mile an hour. Think you can keep up with it, Sidney?'

'Ha ha, very funny.'

'Seriously. Apparently it's been trying to run away since it got on the boat at Costa Rica. But you just have to pick it up and move it back to its basket every day or so. The crew named it Houdini.'

He righted the basket with his foot and then lifted Houdini back inside.

'The boss around?' Peep asked.

'No. There's urgent business on tonight,' Sidney said quietly. 'You'll be needed too. Come on.'

Woody and Peep followed Sidney, carrying the basket between them. The path was empty again.

Gez hissed in the darkness, 'Should we follow?'

'Yes,' Ali said. 'They'll lead us straight to Miss Osborne. Getting rid of her must be their urgent business. We have to stop them!'

The van was already at the end of the lane by the time they had tugged their bikes out of the bushes. They leapt on and pedalled hard. The van pulled away from them, its red lights glowing demon-eyed in the darkness. Ali's legs went up and down like Nan's sewing machine on full power. He was desperate to keep the van in sight.

'It's headed towards the pet shop,' Ali gasped. 'Not far now.'

They did their best to keep up, but it was no good; the van was too fast and soon it had disappeared into the night. Ali hoped that his guess about where they were heading was right.

The three bikes sailed around the final corner and drew up outside the pet shop. It was in total darkness, locked up for the night.

'We should hide the bikes,' Caitlin whispered. 'We

can't let them know we're here.'

'Too right,' Gez said.

'There's garages in the lane behind. Let's see if we can use one of them.' Ali wheeled his bike to the end of the row and then swerved into the lane. There was a narrow gap between the garages and the neigh-bouring hedge. A gap just big enough for three bikes lined up in a row. They stashed them quickly, then turned down the lane, heading towards the back of the pet shop.

They walked the final few metres on tiptoe, so as not to make a noise. But the pet shop was as dark and empty at the back as it was at the front. A white van was parked in the yard.

'There they are!' Caitlin said.

Ali ran over to it and laid his palm on the bumper. 'The engine's warm,' he said. 'It's only just been turned off.' He ran his hands along the side panel, feeling the raised lettering, now painted over. 'It's them, all right. But where have they gone? The pet shop looks deserted.'

'Look!' Caitlin pointed to the house next door: Miss Osborne's house. There was light spilling from an upstairs window, casting long shadows across the back garden. 'They've gone next door. Ali, you were right! They *are* using Miss Osborne's house.'

'Oh, that's evil,' Gez said. 'Keeping her prisoner in her own home. No wonder they were so angry when they saw us sneaking in the garden.'

'Well, they're stealing animals from their habitats and bringing them to cold, rainy gardens in Britain. I don't think they're winning any Mary Poppins awards for kindness any time soon,' Caitlin said.

'We have to go and investigate the house,' Gez said.

'Should we call the police now? They're pretty redhanded in there. With Houdini and Miss Osborne and everything,' Caitlin said.

Ali could see Gez grinning in the moonlight. 'Do we have to?' Gez said. 'I mean, I know we do, but can't we solve the whole mystery first? You know, rescue Miss Osborne, save the sloth, that kind of thing. Then call the police to deliver the criminals gift-wrapped with that rope you've brought?'

Ali thought for a moment. It would be cool to beat the gang on their own. And there was another reason why he didn't want to go to the police just yet. If Dave was in the house, then was Mum too? Would the police arrest her as an accessory? Saving Mum was the most important thing here.

'OK,' he said firmly. 'Let's check it out.'

There was a sudden sound. A door opening. Low voices. Coming from Miss Osborne's house.

'Hide!'

The three dived towards the big industrial bin. There was just enough room for them to duck down behind it, out of sight. They froze. Ali heard footsteps and the flick of a cigarette lighter. Then van doors opened and slammed. An engine started. With a crunch of gears, the van edged down the lane. It was gone.

Ali breathed again. 'How many were there? In the van.'

Gez shrugged. 'I couldn't see.'

'Well,' said Caitlin, 'there's at least one fewer baddy inside. That has to be good news.'

Ali nodded. 'Right. Let's get them.'

They stepped into Miss Osborne's back garden. Ali felt his skin tingle. Were there murderers inside the house? Was there a puma on the loose? Was Mum still safe? At the back door he took a deep breath. 'Ready?' The others nodded. He gripped the handle and turned it. It didn't move. 'It's locked!' he whispered.

Caitlin looked down at the floor. A plastic mat was laid on the concrete, for people to wipe their feet on. She shooed Ali off it, then lifted the corner. A few disturbed woodlice scurried for cover. And there, under a layer of grime, was a key. 'It's where my gran keeps her spare,' Caitlin grinned. She took the key and turned it silently in the lock.

The back door opened into the kitchen – just like at Gez's house. The room was dark and deserted. A huge fridge hummed gently in the corner. The green light of a dishwasher winked at them. In the side wall, a door stood ajar. It was the connecting door into the pet shop. Ali peered inside. It was dark and musty-smelling. The same supplies they'd seen before were piled up against the walls. There was no sign of anyone in the storeroom.

Gez opened the kitchen door leading out into the hall. They were scarcely breathing now, they were trying to be so quiet. Then – yuck! Despite his shallow breaths, Ali couldn't help inhaling the stink that hung around the hallway like a putrid mist. It was dis-gusting! Like the bottoms of cages in the zoo, or, actu-ally, just like bottoms. He struggled to hold in a cough. He forced his feet to take another step.

He moved slowly. The living-room door was on his left; it was closed. The stairs were on his right; the smell got stronger as he got closer to them. He paused outside the living room. Was there anyone in there? Or had Peep, Sidney and Woody gone to meet Dave somewhere else? He pressed his ear against the wood. There was a strange noise coming from inside, a low growl so deep that it was more of a feeling than a sound. The hairs on the back of his neck bristled.

Caitlin edged closer too, and her hair tickled his face as she listened.

'Anyone there?' Gez whispered behind them.

Ali turned and gestured back towards the kitchen. They followed. Ali led them into the quiet darkness of the storeroom. He shut the door gently behind them.

'It's not *someone*,' Ali said quietly. 'But it is *something*. Something growly.'

'A dog?' Gez asked. 'Do you think it's guarding Miss Osborne?'

'Was it Falcon?' Caitlin asked hopefully.

Ali shook his head. That wasn't a dog he had heard; it wasn't anything he recognised. He suddenly imagined a black bear rising up from a flowery sofa to take an angry swipe at them. Was there a bear in the living room? This was way too weird.

'Should we try to rescue it, whatever it is?' Caitlin asked doubtfully.

'It might eat us. It might not realise that we want to help it. I think we should see what else is here. We can come back to rescue it later,' Ali whispered.

'You mean go upstairs? Where that smell is coming from? We'll all puke and then we'll get caught,' Gez said.

'We have to go up,' Ali said.

'Why? Do you think Dave's up there?' Gez asked.

'Dad?' Caitlin said. 'He's not going to be. He's out with Ali's mum, remember. He has an alibi! And I've told you, he loves animals. He wouldn't be involved in anything like this.'

'Hah!' Ali said.

'He wouldn't. You take that back!' Caitlin's voice was more than a whisper.

'Right,' Gez said, standing in between them, 'that's enough. In case you haven't noticed, we're sort of in danger here. Bad guys? Scary beasts? Ring any bells? I know you're both cross, but this isn't the time. We have to save Miss Osborne and get out of here. Save the row for later, OK?'

Ali nodded slowly. Caitlin shrugged.

'Right,' Gez said. 'Back into the house. Up the stairs. Save everyone who needs it. Call the police. Is that a plan, or what?'

'Sure,' Ali said. 'Let's go.'

CHAPTER 30

They left the dark safety of the storeroom. Ali led the way past the hall table and front door, then up the stairs. He was careful not to put his feet in the middle of the steps so that they wouldn't creak. The other two followed silently.

The smell grew stronger as they climbed. It was hot in Ali's nose, like pepper or cumin. And then he heard the noises. Low grunts, squeaks, scratching. It was hard to work out where it was coming from. Then he realised that it was coming from *everywhere*, from behind each of the doors upstairs. He looked around. There were four doors leading off the upstairs landing. The smells and sounds seemed to soak into the air around them, filling the space. Ali felt his legs tremble slightly as the urge to run raced through him. He felt like a rabbit with a hawk circling in the sky above.

There was danger everywhere here – from the animals they could hear but not see, from the gang who had brought the animals here, and from D.O., who might prove to be the most dangerous of all.

Ali took a deep breath through his mouth. He had to keep control.

He moved to the first door and pressed his ear against the wood. There was a faint noise, a kind of scratching twitter. Whatever it was, it wasn't human. He gripped the handle. It turned smoothly. He opened the door a crack. It was dark inside. If there were no lights on, then there were probably no people inside. He hoped. His heart thumped as he pushed the door open. Gez and Caitlin tiptoed behind him.

In the darkness, Ali could make out the outline of a table. There were objects on the table, each covered with a cloth; domes, cubes, cylinders. The noises came from these shapes. He walked forwards carefully, his arms outstretched, tapping at the air to make sure he didn't bump into anything. He knew there were things underneath the cloths: living things. He felt the skin on his arms shiver and rise into goosebumps. Was this really happening to him?

His fingers reached the largest dome. He felt the cloth that covered it; it was thick and luxurious, like velvet.

'Go on,' Gez whispered.

Ali grasped the cloth and then lifted it gently. The scratching sound stopped as though the animal beneath was surprised by the sudden pale dawn.

'What is it?' Caitlin said urgently.

Ali tried to focus in the gloom, but it was no good. He could feel that there was something staring back at him, out of the blackness, but he couldn't tell what it was. 'Torch!' he said.

Caitlin swung the bag off her shoulder and reached inside. Then a thin beam of light shone out across the floor. The beam was shaking, as though the person holding it was very nervous. She brought the beam up. The material in Ali's hand was blood red, and there, glaring out at him from the cage, was the biggest bird he had ever seen. He gasped.

'Wow,' Gez said softly. 'What is it?'

'An eagle. Amazing,' Ali said. The eagle's eyes were focused on him. It had a proud, almost angry look. Its curved ice-pick beak shone in the torchlight.

'It's beautiful,' Caitlin said.

The eagle opened its beak. Ali saw a sudden flash of bright pink tongue before it screeched.

Ali dropped the cloth. Caitlin flicked off the torch. But the sound of the eagle's piercing cry seemed to echo around the room, bouncing off shadows.

'Bums,' Gez muttered.

There was a sound outside the door. Footsteps. Ali looked around, hardly able to make out anything in the sudden dark.

'Bed,' Caitlin said. She grabbed his arm and pulled. Gez followed. She dropped to the floor and rolled, tucking herself under the single bed. Ali copied her, with Gez not far behind. There wasn't much space for the three of them, and Ali could feel the other two breathing on either side of him.

The door opened. Then the main light came on and its sudden brightness was blinding. Ali screwed his eyes tight and listened. Someone with heavy shoes clomped into the room. Then a second pair, lighter. There was a pause and then a voice said, 'It's nothing, Boss. Just that stupid bird.'

Boss!

The boss was here. But was it Dave?

Ali felt Caitlin wriggling. She was squished up against the wall, with the bed just above her. Had she recognised her dad's footsteps?

The light flicked off and Ali heard the pair leave the room.

He took a deep breath, trying to slow his breathing. He tasted the dry dust under the bed and struggled to hold in a cough.

173

For a moment, there was silence.

'At least two of the gang are still here then,' Gez whispered.

'Was it . . . Did you recognise either of them?' Ali asked quietly.

Caitlin shook her head furiously. 'One of them was Woody. I recognised his voice. I don't know who the other person was.'

'Can we get out from here?' Gez asked.

'Shh!' Caitlin whispered.

There was a new sound. Ali could feel it vibrating the floorboards under his back. Footsteps – coming up the stairs! He concentrated hard.

There were lots of people climbing the stairs, three or four maybe! A door opened somewhere.

'Hello, Boss,' Ali heard Sidney say on the landing.

'Who on earth is *she*?' a voice replied. A woman.

'Dunno. We had to bring her. We found them together. We did like you asked with him, we arranged the accident. But we wasn't sure what to do with her. So we brought her here. Sorry, Boss,' Sidney said.

Boss? Boss was a woman? Ali strained to hear more.

'You were supposed to be out tying up loose ends, not making more problems. What am I supposed to do with her?' the woman said.

Then Ali heard a sound that sent shafts of ice into

his heart. A woman cried out as though she had been hurt. And he recognised the cry. It was Mum. The gang had captured Mum! It felt to Ali as though the floor had turned to jelly. Caitlin's hand reached for his.

'Oh, honestly!' Boss said. 'I can't believe you sometimes. Tie her up while I think about this. But you got rid of him, like I told you?'

'Yes, Boss. Permanently. He won't be sticking his nose in where it's not wanted again,' Sidney said.

Ali heard them all moving along the landing and into the furthest bedroom. Then, *slam*, the door shut. Ali felt sick.

'Who was that they've got?' Gez whispered.

Ali lay still. He felt Caitlin squeeze his hand, but he couldn't speak.

'Well, whoever it is,' Gez said, 'they're in big trouble.'

Caitlin reached over Ali's body to give Gez a prod.

'Ow. What was that for?' he hissed.

'Because you're an idiot. That was Ali's mum. And they must have been talking about my dad too.'

'Oh,' Gez said. 'I didn't know. Sorry.'

Ali took a deep breath, then spoke softly. 'She was with Dave tonight. And now she's here. I don't understand.'

Caitlin shook her head. 'My dad isn't the boss. He

175

never was. I told you so. You should have listened.' She let go of his hand. 'Did you hear what they said? They've got rid of him *permanently*. What do they mean?'

No one spoke.

Ali could feel Caitlin, lying rigid, next to him. He knew he had to say something. Anything.

'I'm sorry,' he whispered.

Caitlin didn't reply.

'This is my fault,' Ali said. 'If I'd have listened to you, then we could have been protecting Mum and Dave. She wouldn't have been captured. Caitlin, I'm so sorry.'

Caitlin twisted towards him. 'I don't need sorry. I need action. Hiding under a bed isn't going to rescue anyone. These people hurt my dad and your mum and all these animals. I say it stops, and it stops right now!'

Ali looked at Caitlin. Even in the dark he could see her eyes flashing. She was right. 'Yes! We call the police right now. And these guys will be busted.'

'All right!' Gez said. 'Now we rescue your parents as well as all these animals. Proper superhero style. What are we waiting for?'

He wriggled out from under the bed. Ali and Caitlin followed. Ali put his hand into his back pocket and pulled out his phone. He pressed a key to light up the screen. Nothing. The screen stayed black. 'Shine the torch,' he said. Caitlin flashed the beam over the phone. The screen was cracked. The case was loose. The phone was broken.

'I must have landed on it when I fell off your roof,' Ali whispered.

They looked at each other in the torchlight. Phoneless. In a building stuffed with wild animals and bad guys. And a bad girl. There was a lump in Ali's throat that he had a hard time swallowing down.

'What are we going to do?' Caitlin said.

'There's only one thing we can do. We have to get out and call from a phone box,' Ali said.

'But what about Dad and your mum? We haven't got enough time! There must be a phone in the house,' Caitlin said fiercely.

Gez nodded. 'Yes, in the hall, or the main bedroom. I bet we could call from there.'

Ali thought about it, trying to remember – had he seen a phone downstairs? There had been a small table next to the front door with an ugly vase of dried flowers. And there had been something else – a small black box with wires attached. 'Cordless phone,' he said finally. 'There was a holder for a cordless phone downstairs. But the phone was missing.'

'It could be anywhere,' Caitlin said.

'No, it will be with the boss. She's in control of everything,' Ali said, trying to keep the anger out of his voice.

The boss. It wasn't Dave – he'd been totally wrong about that. He remembered the voice. *Tie her up.* Talking about *Mum*. Like some witch from a fairy story. He shivered. 'Caitlin, what's Miss Osborne's first name?'

'I know,' Gez said. 'Remember the pizza receipt in their pooey bin? She's called Donna.'

Donna Osborne.

D.O.

Miss Osborne hadn't been kidnapped or murdered. She was the ringleader!

It was as though the ceiling was crashing down around him. *Thump.* A weight of guilt landing on him. His face burned. He'd been an idiot. All this time he'd been suspecting Dave, but it turned out that Dave had been making trouble for the gang. Dave was one of the good guys. If only he'd believed Caitlin, then perhaps he and Mum wouldn't be in danger now.

'Caitlin, I'm sorry,' he said. 'The boss must be Miss Osborne. Donna Osborne. She has to be the "D.O." on the note we found, not your dad at all.'

Caitlin nodded slowly. 'Ali Desai Ferguson, my dad is in deep trouble. Did you hear what they said? A permanent accident. I don't care about your sorry. I care about finding him and saving him. OK?'

'OK. I just wanted to say –'

'Well don't,' Caitlin interrupted. 'Just help me save him.'

'Hey,' Gez interrupted. 'You two are fighting like you're already brother and sister! It's brilliant. Your parents should totally get married. If they don't get murdered first.'

'Gez!' Ali hissed. Gez really was about as sensitive as a lamp post. But he did have a point. They needed to rescue Mum and find Dave. And to do that, they needed to get to a phone. He just hoped there was enough time.

'Let's move,' Ali said. 'I bet the phone's in the front bedroom with Miss Osborne. Peep, Sidney and Woody are in there too. How can we get past them with only the three of us?'

Gez shook his head. 'There aren't just three of us. There's an eagle right here. And somewhere there's a bear and a sloth and who knows what else. We just need to recruit them to our cause.'

'OK, Doctor Dolittle,' Caitlin said. 'How exactly are you going to do that?'

'Easy. I just make sure the cages are pointing at the bad guys when I open the doors.'

CHAPTER 31

'Fine,' Ali said. 'Gez, take the eagle. Then let's see what other animals we can find.'

Gez lifted the cage from the table as gently as he could. He wrapped both arms around it to steady it. Inside, the eagle scrabbled, doing its best to stay upright, but it didn't screech. Ali lifted the cloth on another cage; ten or twenty small birds whirred and fluttered over each other to get away from the pale light. They would do nicely. Ali picked up their cage. Their tiny wingbeats fluttered like the butterflies in his stomach.

Caitlin, with their bag of supplies slung over her shoulder, opened the bedroom door. The landing was empty. Ali crept out, clutching his cage. Caitlin and Gez followed behind. Caitlin pressed her ear against the next door along and waited. She opened it slowly.

The bathroom. There were no people inside, but there was something in the bathtub. Another cage with a cloth thrown over it. She tiptoed up to it, lifted the corner and dropped it with a squeak of surprise. 'It's a crocodile!' she whispered.

Ali squatted next to her and looked inside. 'No, it's a monitor lizard. Cool. Their bite has more bacteria than a toilet bowl.'

'Yuck.' Caitlin grabbed the top of the cage and heaved it out of the tub. The lizard tried to turn, its tail flicking angrily back and forth. Caitlin shuddered, but held on tight.

'Come on,' Ali said, and waved them out towards the front bedroom. Here, they lined the three cages up, like cannons aimed at an enemy ship. Then Ali leaned forwards and gently unhooked the latches that kept the cages closed.

He whispered instructions quickly. 'Caitlin, look for a phone. Gez, release any other animals. I'll get Mum. Ready?' Everyone nodded. He leaned forwards and opened the cage doors.

The animals didn't move.

'Come on!' Gez tapped their cages to persuade them out.

Just then, a loud bark came from somewhere nearby. Falcon! The sound of the dog seemed to galvanise the captive animals. The eagle's shriek tore the air into pieces. The lizard scuttled forwards, the clattering of its claws on the bottom of the cage sounding like someone pounding on an old-fashioned typewriter. The small birds whirled like a mini-tornado.

The bedroom door flew open. 'Wha—' Peep yelled. The eagle flew upwards, its talons extended. Peep leapt backwards. The lizard hurtled between his legs. The small birds, brilliant in reds and golds and greens, darted at his face, desperate to avoid the eagle. Peep tripped and fell back into the room with the eagle screeching and swooping above him.

Ali ran right over Peep, treading on his belly. Caitlin and Gez were right behind him. He looked around: a woman stood open-mouthed in the centre of the room. Her blonde hair was wrapped in an elaborate knot on top of her head, her skin was tanned and her lipstick was bright red. *Miss Osborne*, Ali thought. The next second, Miss Osborne screamed as the thick legs of the monitor lizard hauled themselves up her skirt; Woody and Sidney crouched low as the eagle screamed at them, Sidney yelling as the spiralling bird slashed his cheek.

And Mum?

There she was, struggling, bound to a chair, her eyes wide with alarm. A piece of tape was stuck over her mouth. Ali ran over to her and pulled the tape free.

'Ali? What are –'

'Shh, Mum. Let me get you out of here.' Ali crouched down behind the chair. The knot that held her arms in place was complicated. He worked at it desperately, tugging this way and that. The screams of the people and the animals continued around him like a rising symphony, but he concentrated on freeing Mum. Right now nothing else mattered.

'Ali!' Caitlin cried. He looked up and saw Miss Osborne heading for the door. The lizard had scratched her legs and torn the bottom of her skirt, but hadn't stopped her.

Just then Falcon rushed forwards with a torrent of barking. She stood in the doorway, blocking the exit, and barked at Miss Osborne with her teeth on full display.

'Falcon! Sweetie!' Miss Osborne jumped back in alarm.

Gez threw himself across the floor and rugby-tackled the women to the ground. 'Smashdown!' he yelled.

Falcon turned her attention to Peep, who was struggling to get up. She growled and he cringed back down, shielding his face.

'Good girl, Falcon!' Caitlin yelled.

Ali looked over at Caitlin. She was sitting on the bed with a phone cradled against her chin. She had stopped talking in order to praise Falcon, but there was definitely someone on the other end: she must have got through to the police.

The rope was loosened at last. Mum stood up, rubbing her wrists. 'Watch out!' she shouted.

Woody made a grab for Ali, but the lizard, distressed by the sudden movement, leapt into the air and sank its teeth into Woody's arm. Woody yelped and spun around. Ali grabbed the rope and threw the other end to Mum. She understood. Together they ran around Sidney and Woody, looping the rope around the struggling pair. Blood ran down Sidney's face in gory streams. Woody sobbed, still trying to shake the lizard off. Ali pulled tight on the rope and both men were tugged together, trapped, with the rope around their middles. He tied the biggest knot he could manage.

Gez was struggling to keep Miss Osborne under control. She was bigger than him and fought furiously. He had her in a headlock, then he didn't, then he did again. Ali was glad that Gez had his big brothers to practice wrestling with; otherwise he would have had no chance.

Caitlin put down the phone. 'They're on their way!' she said. Then she went to help Gez, gripping Miss

Osborne's arms, so Gez could sit on her legs. Finally, unable to move, the woman stopped struggling. Ali threw them the spare rope from the hold-all, and together Caitlin and Gez tied Miss Osborne to Peep, who still hadn't got up.

The small birds fluttered to find perches. A few landed on Sidney, who was too stunned to even shake them off. The eagle settled on top of a wardrobe, glaring down at everyone. It was then that Ali noticed the sloth, moving slowly away from its basket towards the door. He grinned. Houdini might just make it this time.

'Mum, are you all right?' Ali asked.

Mum's bottom lip looked a bit wobbly and her mascara was smeared, but she smiled as best she could. 'Yes, I'm OK. Thanks to you three. How did you know I was here?'

'We didn't,' Ali said. 'We thought Dave might be here.'

Caitlin looked up. 'Where is Dad?' she asked. 'Did he go home?'

Mum gasped. 'He's not with you? Oh no.'

'What happened?' Caitlin said, her voice high and anxious.

'They caught us outside your flat. We'd had dinner and a walk, and were just going back for a coffee. But *they* were waiting outside the door.' Mum pointed to Woody and Peep. 'They seemed surprised that I was there. They were only after your dad. They said he'd poked his nose into their business once too often.'

'What did they do to him?' Caitlin said.

'Oh, love, I don't know.' Mum's voice cracked and her eyes filled. 'It was all so quick. They put some kind of cloth over my mouth. Then it all went black and I woke up here.'

'But what about Dad?' Caitlin insisted.

Mum shook her head. 'I haven't seen him here. We were outside your flat. I don't know. But wherever he is, he's in danger. These guys mean business. I dread to think what would have happened to me if you three hadn't arrived.'

Caitlin's face seemed to flick through emotions: worry, dread, anger. Then it froze on anger. She looked at Miss Osborne, who struggled on the floor, trying to loosen the rope around her arms.

Caitlin held her firmly and leaned in close. 'Where's my dad?' she said in a voice that made Ali shiver.

There was no answer.

The room filled with the sound of sirens and strobing blue light from the street below. The police had arrived. The front door burst open and what seemed like hundreds of booted feet charged into the house. Caitlin shook Miss Osborne's shoulders. 'Where's my dad?' she yelled again.

'Taken care of,' Miss Osborne said. 'He's been on my trail for weeks. Woody tried to teach him a lesson, then we came after you. He came to his senses then, gave Falcon back, said he'd keep quiet. But it was too little too late. Well, he's learned now that you don't mess with Donna Osborne and get away with it.'

Caitlin starred at Miss Osborne, her eyes wild with anger. Ali stepped forwards, ready to pull Caitlin back.

Suddenly, the landing clattered with the sound of footsteps. The room filled with police officers and noise – radio chatter, shouts, instructions. The eagle took off again and resumed its screeching.

'No one move!' an officer yelled.

'But my dad –' Caitlin edged towards the door.

'Wait.' A second officer held Caitlin by the shoulder.

'My dad's still out there somewhere. He's –'

'Don't worry, we'll call your dad for you,' the first officer interrupted.

'No, you don't understand. Please, listen. We have to find him.'

'I'm sure your dad will understand. Go sit on the bed, and I'll find a nice lady officer to sit with you till all this is sorted.'

'No, listen –' Caitlin tried again.

'I'll find a lady officer in just a minute.'

Caitlin looked stunned. Ali quietly picked up the hold-all and nodded towards the door. They all three tried to slip past the policemen.

'Where are you kids going? We'll need to take statements from everyone,' the officer said crossly.

'I can't stay in here,' Ali said. 'It . . . It stinks. Lizard poo. Need air. Gonna be sick.' He made disgusting retching noises into his palm.

The officer's nose crinkled in horror. 'Go on then. But don't go far. We'll need to talk to you.'

They ran past the police, down the stairs and through the kitchen, with Falcon bounding at their heels. Gez shut the back door gently behind them.

CHAPTER 32

The air outside was delicious, fresh and cold. Ali took great lungfuls. Mum was safe. But Dave wasn't. They had to find him. Caitlin had already grabbed her bike from its hiding place. Ali and Gez followed suit. Then they were pedalling as hard as they could, bouncing over potholes and churning loose stones into the air. Falcon ran alongside, panting, with her tongue lolling out of the side of her mouth.

Caitlin kept ahead of them the whole way back to the flats, and she was the first to toss her bike aside at the main door and rush into the building.

Ali followed. He had a heavy feeling in his heart.

Caitlin slammed her palm against the lift call button, willing it to come quickly. Ali, Gez and Falcon reached her just as the doors opened and they all piled in together. Caitlin hit '14' and the lift rose.

'What if he's not there?' Gez asked.

Caitlin stood stock-still; she didn't answer.

'If he's not there,' Ali said, 'then we look for him. And we find him.'

Caitlin smiled gratefully.

The lift came to a stop and the doors opened. The corridor in front of them was lit only by small yellow lights set above the front doors. The space between the lights was in dark shadow. Caitlin ran out of the lift to her flat. She opened the door and rushed inside. 'Dad? Dad?' she shouted. Then she came back out. 'He isn't here,' she said. Ali could hear the tears in her voice.

'Don't panic,' he said, taking hold of her arm to steady her. 'They can't have taken him far. He'd have shouted the whole way, and people would have heard.' Ali felt Falcon's warm, furry body lean against him. He had an idea. 'Falcon, find Dave,' he said.

Falcon looked up at him, her head cocked to one side as though she was thinking.

'Come on, Falcon. Dave – fetch.'

'She can't do it,' Caitlin said. 'You know she's daft.'

'No, she was on our side back there. Against Miss Osborne. She can do it. Caitlin, give her something of his to smell.'

Caitlin grabbed one of Dave's coats and held it under Falcon's nose. 'Find Dad,' she said in a shaky voice.

Falcon gave a little bark, then she sniffed the air. Her tail wagged gently, then more vigorously. She took a few steps one way, and back the other way, sniffing all the time. She barked again, before setting off down the hall with determination.

'She's found something!' Gez said. 'She's going to the roof!'

Caitlin followed Falcon, with Ali and Gez not far behind, up towards the roof access.

With Falcon nosing eagerly at the door Caitlin leaned against it, pushing it open. Instantly, the stairwell filled with a cold wind, sharp against their faces. Up on the roof, the city cast an orange glow into the sky, hiding the stars.

'Is he here?' Gez said.

Ali looked around. Black shadows draped over the rooftop like shrouds. There could be anything crouching in the darkness, watching them. Ali blinked, clearing the tears that the cold wind had whipped up.

'There!' Caitlin shouted. She and Falcon bounded forward together. Something lay on the concrete. Something large and still.

Dave.

His eyes were closed and his skin looked pale and waxy.

'Dad? Dad!' Caitlin shook his shoulders. Dave made no sound.

'Caitlin,' Ali said, 'give Gez your keys. Gez, go to Caitlin's flat and call an ambulance.'

Caitlin's hand shook as she handed over the keys. Gez sped away, without looking back.

'Dad?' Caitlin whispered. He didn't move. Ali saw a tear fall from her face and splash on to Dave's cheek. They were too late.

Dave's eyelids flickered.

He moaned gently.

He was still alive! Ali felt a rush of something through his body, a warm gladness that made his own heart leap.

'Caitlin! It's OK, he's not dead!' He knelt next to Dave. 'Dave, can you hear me? Dave?'

Dave whispered something. It was so soft that it was hardly more than a sigh. Then, he repeated it, louder. 'Anita?'

Ali gasped in surprise. Dave was injured, maybe near to death, and the first thing he asked about was Mum. 'It's OK. Mum's OK. We found her.'

Dave smiled. Then he gasped. His breathing was ragged now, as though the pain was growing.

'Dad? Where does it hurt? What did they do?'

'Sn . . . sn . . . uck,' Dave whispered. Then a horrible

juddering ran through him, as though electric currents had been slammed on.

'Dad!' Caitlin's scream tore the air.

'Caitlin,' Ali said firmly, 'he said "snake". At least, I think he did.'

Dave's body shook and trembled. Time was running out.

'Quick. Look for a bite.' Ali bent down to start looking.

Caitlin made a strangled noise in her throat but didn't move.

'Caitlin, listen. Your dad will be OK, but only if we act fast. First aid. Look for the bite. Now!'

'I can't see, it's too dark.'

Ali remembered the bag he had been clinging on to: the torch! He grabbed it and switched it on. In the beam of light, Dave's face looked worse. His skin was the colour of sour milk and he was covered in a thin film of sweat. Whatever the venom was doing to him, it was serious.

Caitlin ran her fingers gently over Dave's face, checking every inch of his skin. Nothing. She moved down, Ali keeping the torch trained closely on her moving hands.

'Here!' Caitlin had reached Dave's arms. She held his right arm cradled in her own. Ali could see straight away what she meant. The wrist was thick and swollen like a side of ham. Two bright red puncture marks throbbed in the centre of the swelling. The skin around the marks looked ragged.

'What is it?' Caitlin said.

'I knew it,' Ali said. 'Look at those two holes. He's been bitten. Something deadly, by the looks of it.'

'What should we do? Could we suck the poison out?'

Ali thought about the *Giant Atlas of World Animals*; Chapter 4: Australia. There was an information box about snakes. He knew what to do! 'No. You have to bandage it up tight, to stop the poison spreading. And keep him very still.'

Caitlin pulled off her cardigan and pulled it taut against her dad's skin, wrapping it securely around the bite. She was just in a T-shirt now, and the cold wind was making her shiver.

'The blanket too. Here.' Ali rifled through the bag and pulled out the small picnic blanket. Caitlin lay it over Dave, tucking the edges around him as though he was the child. She looked up. 'Ali, that man, Sidney, wanted this to look like an accident.'

Ali looked at Caitlin. What was she getting at? Then he realised. If this was an accident, it had to look as though Dave had been bitten by his own snake. Which meant that the snake was still up here, on the roof with them. Ali felt his skin crawl up his spine.

He looked out across the rooftop, looking for a coiled mass preparing to strike. It was no use; it was too dark to make out anything. Every shadow seemed to slither and slide as he peered into it.

He looked down at Dave and Caitlin. It seemed as though Dave was slipping away from them with each faint heartbeat. Caitlin moved back to cradle his head on her lap. Ali took a long, deep breath. When the ambulance got here, they would need to know which antidote to use. They'd only know that if he could show them the snake that bit Dave.

Ali turned out to face the city. The wind had calmed a little and he could hear the sound of a siren. But it was faint. The ambulance was still miles away. He was on his own.

CHAPTER 33

Ali picked up the hold-all. It was much lighter now – the rope was at Miss Osborne's house; Caitlin was using the torch to check the swelling on Dave's arm; the blanket was gone; the tin of dog food must have rolled away somewhere.

He stepped away from Dave.

There was a venomous snake somewhere out here that needed to be caught.

He tipped out the contents of the bag: a tin opener, some biscuits and a bowl. On those TV shows where that man in combat trousers wandered around picking up snakes and crocodiles and things, he always used a stick. He had nothing that was anything like a stick.

And he had to find the snake if there was any chance of saving Dave.

He took slow steps into the darkness beyond

Caitlin's torchlight and looked back. Falcon had laid her head next to Dave's; Caitlin was whispering quietly to him, stroking his forehead. Caitlin and Dave needed him to do this. They needed him to be brave. If he'd trusted Dave in the first place, this might not have happened. This was his only way to say sorry. After all, he couldn't say sorry to a dead man.

He forced his legs to keep moving. This wasn't like looking at pictures of snakes in a book. He imagined fangs gleaming, venom dripping, yellow eyes glaring all around him. Was that a hiss? No, it was the lift machinery whirring into action.

'Here, snakey, snakey,' Ali whispered.

There! Something shining! It was a small cage. Ali approached carefully, not even daring to swallow. He could see through the wire mesh that there was a darkness, a shadow in one corner. Something small, coiled in on itself.

'I found it,' he tried to shout, but the words just croaked out.

The cage door was open. The men must have forced Dave's hand in there and the snake, defending itself, bit him. Then they left the cage for the police to find. He leaned down; the snake was inside the cage, still and silent. Right next to the open door. He was going to have to reach out and close it. He was going to have to put his hand right out where the snake could strike. Near those shiny scales and dripping fangs.

The empty bag! He could use that! He wrapped the thick nylon around his arm, covering his hand, and reached out slowly, his ears straining for an angry hiss. Nothing. The door was just millimetres away. So was the snake. Through the fabric his fingers felt the metal bars. He clawed at the frame. The door swung closed. He pushed home the bolt.

He sank to his knees.

The snake was trapped.

He wasn't done yet. Picking up the cage by the handle, he moved back towards the torchlight and Dave's still body.

'How's he doing?' he asked.

Caitlin looked up, her face grey and tight.

'Don't worry,' Ali said. 'I know he's going to be OK.' He hoped and hoped that what he said would be true. More than anything, he wanted a second chance to get to know Dave properly and to say sorry.

The access door opened. Gez came through, followed by three people in green jumpsuits. They swarmed around Dave, asking Caitlin questions.

Gez came up to Ali. 'What's that you've got?'

Ali held up the cage so Gez could see. A brown-black snake with golden bands lay coiled in the corner.

Gez peered closer. 'Hey!' he yelled. 'Hey, ambulance-people, there's a snake here. Do you want it?'

'It's what did this,' Ali said, pointing to Dave's arm.

Heavy footsteps came towards him. 'Thanks, son. We'll take it to be identified,' a deep voice said. 'Careful. Don't touch it.'

'It's OK,' Gez said. 'I've got a snake at home. That one's asleep now. It's the cold up here, you see. After biting someone, then being left up here, it's knackered. It won't hurt anyone. At least, not till it gets somewhere warmer.'

Ali stared at the cage. The snake was asleep? He shook his head. He should have known that. He'd got more than one thing very wrong tonight, but with luck, he'd be able to make up for it.

'What's up?' Gez asked.

'Nothing,' Ali said, shaking his head. 'Do you think he'll be OK?'

Gez nodded towards the access door. The paramedics were wheeling Dave away on a stretcher, wrapped in a thick blanket. Caitlin walked alongside, gripping the rail.

'Well, they haven't covered his face,' Gez said, 'so I reckon he'll be fine.'

TWO WEEKS LATER

CHAPTER 34

The letter box clattered. Ali stopped struggling with his tie and went to see what was in the post.

A card lay on the mat, a small rectangle with a picture of a sunset and a sandy beach. Ali's breath caught in his throat. He reached down and slowly turned the card over. On one side – the address side – there was lots of cramped writing. Nan had forwarded it from their old address. On the other side – the side for writing your message – there were three lines, scrawled in Dad's handwriting.

Dear Ali,
I saw the sunset on this beach. It was beautiful. What an adventure!
Love, Dad

Ali sighed.

'Hey, sonny,' Dave said behind him. 'Anything interesting?'

Ali turned and smiled up at him. 'It's just a card. Dad's still doing OK.'

'Good. Now you'd better hurry or we're going to be late for this shebang.'

Ali nodded. He rested the card up on top of the heater. It brightened up the hallway, he thought. Then he went to finish getting ready.

The microphone squealed with feedback. The crowd all winced. The sloth in the enclosure didn't seem to notice; it carried on chewing at its pile of leaves.

'First, I'd like to thank you all for coming,' the zoo manager said.

Ali let the rest of the speech roll over him, like blossom in the breeze.

The important thing was that Dave was fine.

Ali had pieced the story together slowly, with Caitlin adding bits as she wheedled them out of her dad.

Dave had suspected that Miss Osborne was smuggling something, but he wasn't sure what. So he'd gone to the river to investigate. He'd heard the eagle shriek inside the crate and realised what was going on. And so he'd been beaten up by Woody. Then the gang had tried to take Caitlin. Dave couldn't run the risk of them succeeding, so he'd given Falcon back and promised to stay away. But that hadn't been enough for Miss Osborne. And so he ended up in a hospital bed.

Now Dave was better, and the animals they'd found at Miss Osborne's were being given a temporary new home.

Ali tugged at the hem of his suit. It felt weird.

'Stay still,' Mum hissed.

He caught her eye; she grinned. Next to her, Dave stood looking proud, with a grin wider than a bus. He had a suit on too, though Ali suspected it might have come off the back of a lorry. The label said Dulcey and Gabana.

'We're here to thank a very brave group of children and to welcome the newest animals to the zoo. Without these children, these animals would have had a very dark future indeed. The animals will be staying with us for a while, until they can be returned to their natural habitats,' the manager said.

Caitlin pinched his arm gently. Ali knew that meant she was pleased. He felt that he knew Dave and Caitlin well now. They hadn't moved in or anything, but Caitlin had stayed with them until Dave was well enough to leave hospital.

Dave was talking about taking them all on holiday

in the summer. Ali had thought about asking to go to Asia, perhaps to go and see monkeys running all over temples, or the view across the Himalayas. He had thought about it for about five seconds. But then he'd seen the huge smile on Mum's face. Dave made her really happy. Ali'd asked to go to France instead.

He hadn't opened his *Giant Atlas of World Animals* for a while. Dave had arranged with his mate at the zoo for Ali to help out at weekends. So Ali hadn't needed to look at the pictures – he had the real thing.

He would never throw away Dad's postcards, or stop wanting to see him again. He knew that. But Mum was right – life went on.

All around them, a crowd was gathered: Grandpa and Nan, Gez's whole family, people from the newspaper.

Everyone clapped as the zoo official finished his speech.

Then it was Ali's turn.

He felt Mum push him forward. Caitlin and Gez came with him too as he mounted the few steps up to the mic. Falcon stayed with Mum and Dave.

'Thanks for coming, everyone,' Ali said into the microphone. He saw Mum wipe a tear from the corner of her eye, though she was still smiling. 'The zoo have asked us to choose a name for the sloth, while he's staying here. We thought about it for a long time. His old name was Houdini, because he always wanted to escape. Well, very soon he'll be free. He'll go back to Costa Rica. So his old name isn't right any more. So we've decided to call him Dave. After one of the nicest men we know.'

This time it was Dave's turn to wipe something from his eye.

Ali continued, 'If I'd have trusted Dave in the first place, then Dave-the-sloth might have been rescued much sooner.'

Caitlin stepped up to the mic. 'But Gez and me are glad that you didn't, because then we wouldn't have fought the baddies. We liked doing that.'

Gez nodded in agreement, but seemed too awed by the crowd to speak.

'I hope Dave-the-sloth will be happy in his new home,' Ali concluded.

The crowd cheered. Ali saw Grandpa shaking Dave's hand and Nan kissing Mum. He felt Caitlin give his hand a little squeeze and his heart swelled inside him, as though it were too big for his chest.

Behind him, Dave-the-sloth closed his eyes and chewed another leaf.

ACKNOWLEDGEMENTS

This book would have floundered before it even got started, if it weren't for my lovely Bath writer-friends; thank you.

Thanks too to Rosemary and Jodie for their advice. Also to Emma M, Talya and Emma B at Bloomsbury for their help on this book and their support this last year.

And of course, to Simon, for all the chuckles.

ABOUT THE AUTHOR

Elen Caldecott wrote her first book, *How Kirsty Jenkins Stole the Elephant*, once she realised it was probably possible to steal anything. With *How Ali Ferguson Saved Houdini*, she wondered whether it was possible to keep a zoo in a terraced house. While writing the book, she decided that the answer to that question is a resounding 'no'.

Elen lives in Bristol with her husband. She has recently moved into a bigger flat, so by the time you read this she will, hopefully, own a dog. It may, or may not, be called Augustus Snags.

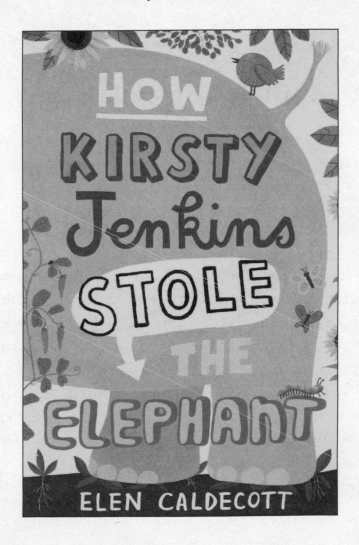

Turn the page to read an extract.

CHAPTER 1

Kirsty stumbled and fell towards the acid-green leaves. As they scratched her face she realised that they were exactly the same colour as the Amazonian poisonous frogs she had seen in the river earlier. She got back to her feet quickly. This was a dangerous place; deadly snakes hunted in the canopy above, jaguars padded through the undergrowth. She stepped forwards carefully so that the ginormous, man-eating beetles couldn't gnaw her boots. One of her fellow explorers had lost his big toe that way only yesterday. Her stomach rumbled. She had been trekking for days and supplies were running low.

'Can I eat some peas, Grandad?' she shouted.

The thump, thump of her grandad's shovel stopped.

'Are you still there? I thought you'd gone home,' said Grandad.

'No. I'm just on an expedition. We've got no food. We might have to resort to cannibalism. So, can I eat some of the peas? Please, please?' Her fingers came to rest on a thick pod right above her left shoulder. She grinned at Grandad, even though she couldn't see him past the wigwam of leaves.

'You're worse than all the birds, slugs and snails put together. I'm amazed I ever have anything to take home from this allotment.' Grandad started shovelling again. 'Go on, then. I wouldn't want you to have to eat any fellow explorers.' Kirsty heard him chuckle.

The pod cracked open between her thumbs. Her tongue teased out each pea and guided it on to her back teeth. Then, *crunch*, her whole mouth flooded with sweetness. She settled down on to her back, looking up through the leaves at the summer-bright sky. Grandad was digging again. She could hear noises on the other plots too: the squeak of a wheelbarrow, the whistle of a kettle boiling on a gas stove, shouts and laughter as people gave each other advice. Everyone was here today, working on their little plot of land. They all grew fruit and vegetables to take home. But none of them did it as well as Grandad. She picked a wodge of chewed pea off her back tooth. If only she could eat Grandad's peas every day! When she ruled the world it would always be summer and peas would

2

grow all the time. And she wouldn't have to share a room with Dawn every weekend, bossing everyone around just because she was the eldest.

Thinking about Dawn made her feel annoyed. She sat up quickly and the leaves scratched her face again. The expedition! She had almost forgotten! Kirsty clapped her hands. Her fellow explorers leapt to attention. She had managed to find them food, scavenged from the unwilling jungle. That would stop the whispers of mutiny. For now. She uncurled the ancient map of Hazdrubal and set a course south. She was either leading them to untold riches, or to certain death. Only time would tell which it was to be. With one hand holding her compass and the other clutching a knife, Kirsty hacked a path through the clinging vines.

'Come on, pet.' The shovelling had stopped. Grandad was just outside her pea wigwam.

'It isn't time to go,' Kirsty said.

'I'm afraid it is. I promised your dad I'd have you home early today. It's the weekend. Ben and Dawn will be at your house soon. You never know, you might even have fun with your brother and sister.'

'Half-sister,' Kirsty muttered. Dad was Ben and Dawn's dad too, but they had a different mum. Dad had been married to their mum once, but then he had

3

married Kirsty's mum. At weekends they came to Kirsty's house. Ben was nice, but Dawn was a total pain. When she wasn't there, Kirsty and Dad would do nice things together, like listen to Dad's records or watch Kirsty's DVDs, or even just rearrange their collections. But when Dawn was there, she moaned and yelled and spoiled everything.

Kirsty curled up inside the plants. It was a tight squeeze, though she knew that Grandad had planted them wide apart just so she could keep on using her den. She rested her head on the ground. It smelled of warm earth and the tang of leaves. A few weeds had grown up among the peas. She pulled one out of the ground, its silvery roots and all.

'If you don't come out, I'll have to come in and get you!' Grandad said.

Kirsty started giggling despite herself. She knew what was coming. Grandad was going to get her to move the way he always did – with lots of laughing and screaming. His hand reached in and grabbed her bare foot. His rough fingertips tickled and tickled her sole until she cried with laughter.

'Stop it! Stop it!' she yelled. Now there would be a twisting tug-of-war as she tried to break free. She yanked her leg. Grandad's grip loosened. Her foot sprang back towards her. He had let go. Grandad

4

had let go on the first tug! That wasn't right. Kirsty frowned.

Cough, cough, cough.

It sounded like Grandad was coughing from some place deep, deep inside. It sounded like it hurt. Kirsty struggled out through the plants.

'Grandad?'

He was bent over, coughing into his huge white handkerchief. At the sound of her voice, Grandad looked up. His eyes were all watery. 'I'm fine, pet. Right as rain.' But he struggled to get the words out.

Kirsty shivered, despite the sunlight.